CU00860335

The Curious Cousins and the Smugglers of Bligh Island

The Curious Cousins, Volume 1

Alex R Carver

Published by Alex R Carver, 2021.

THE CURIOUS COUSINS AND THE SMUGGLERS OF BLIGH ISLAND

First edition. May 4, 2021.

Copyright © 2021 Alex R Carver.

ISBN: 979-8201040567

Written by Alex R Carver.

1

Sunlight, warm and golden yellow, shone down from the cloudless sky, offering a promise of the heat to come, while gulls flew back and forth across the unmarred blue, their cries blending into something almost musical.

Every so often a gull would dive, disappearing beneath the shallow waves briefly before soaring back into the sky. Most had wriggling fish in their beaks, which they carried away to eat, while those that were unsuccessful returned to circling and wheeling in search of a target.

Ordinarily, Edward would have been watching the aerial display avidly. He was a lover of all things in nature, except spiders, he couldn't stand the ugly, evil-looking things. He hated them so much that he had once run from a room with a girlish scream at the sight of a particularly large specimen.

Just then, however, he was indifferent to the show nature was putting on. His attention was elsewhere.

The gentle breeze that ruffled his wavy, dirty-blond hair and plucked at his t-shirt was ignored as thoroughly as his surroundings. The only thing the fifteen-year-old had eyes for was the speck on the horizon; only it wasn't a speck anymore.

The ferry that bore him was far from speedy, yet the small island that was his destination drew steadily closer, seeming to double in size with each passing second.

Edward's grey eyes remained fixed on the island as it grew from a dot to a blob and then began to take on the outline of something that might be inhabited by humans, though its irregular shape showed no sign of occupation yet.

It wasn't until the ferry had been underway for half an hour that the finger reaching up from the island into the sky became identifiable. At first, it had appeared to be nothing more than a column of rock pointing to the heavens from atop a cliff, but now he could see that it was a lighthouse, standing tall and upright like a sentry, guarding the island against intruders.

The next sign of human habitation came into view ten minutes later as a small bay, containing the island's only town, revealed itself when the ferry curved around the island.

Details were hard to make out at that distance, but Edward pictured white-washed houses, a pub, a small shop, a church, and not much else.

His mental picture depressed him.

It would be bad enough visiting for a day, he thought. Spending the summer holidays there with relatives he had never met was likely to be a nightmare.

"Is that it?"

Edward didn't hear the question, just as he hadn't heard the footsteps of the questioner. It wasn't until he was tapped on the shoulder that he became aware there was anyone with him in the bow of the ferry.

Looking around, he saw two girls standing behind him.

The grey eyes of his sister, Elizabeth, who was the taller of the pair, alternated between Edward and the approaching island.

Anyone seeing them together would have been forgiven for thinking they were twins. Most people assumed they were, given the similarities in their appearances. They were not twins, though, almost eleven months separated them, with Edward being the elder.

The second girl, Henrietta, who preferred to be known as Henri, was a cousin rather than a sister. She was both younger and shorter than the other two, being only thirteen and barely five-foot-tall, compared to their five-feet-seven and five-feet-five.

Height was not the only difference between the cousins. Henri's hair was a golden sheet of pure blonde with no trace of darkness, and her eyes were a brilliant blue rather than the cloudy grey of Edward and Elizabeth. She was also dressed more casually in a pair of denim shorts made from jeans whose legs had been cut off untidily, and a scruffy and faded red t-shirt, while Edward wore a pair of jeans that looked brand new and a blue t-shirt, and Elizabeth had on a lemon-coloured summer dress.

"What did you say?" Edward asked of his sister.

"I asked if that's it," Elizabeth said, pointing ahead to the cluster of buildings that were taking on individual characteristics as they drew nearer.

"Of course that's it," Henri said, moving past the older pair so she could climb up onto the railing at the very bow of the ferry. She wobbled for a few moments before catching her balance and then leant forward, bracing herself with her legs, as though to see their destination more clearly. "Where else do you think it could be? The ferry only goes between Handley and Bligh Island, they told us that, so that has to be Blighton."

"That it be, girly," a deep rumbling voice said suddenly as a shadow fell across the teens.

At the sound of the voice, the trio spun around. The speaker was a huge, barrel-chested man with an enormous and unkempt, iron-grey beard, eyes that were so deeply set it was impossible to make out their colour, a bald head, and a mass of wrinkles that spoke of a long life spent outdoors.

The ferry's first mate, who looked as though he belonged on a seventeenth-century pirate vessel, had a frightening appearance and smelled unpleasantly of fish and tobacco smoke, but Edward held his ground, though it took an effort. Elizabeth wasn't as brave as her brother, she backed up, wanting to put as much space between herself and the first mate as she could.

Henri was the only one of the three who was undisturbed by the mate's appearance. She looked him over briefly and then turned her attention back to where she was going to be staying for the next six weeks.

"You'd best get down from there, girly. If you're not careful, you'll go overboard. Besides, we'll be there soon."

Henri ignored the advice and tempted fate by leaning even further over the railing. "My name's not girly," she said over her shoulder. She was a confirmed tomboy and hated any suggestion that she was at all like Elizabeth, who was about as girly as a girl could be. "It's Henri."

"Don't encourage him," Elizabeth told her cousin. "You know it's not a good idea to talk to strangers. And get down from there." She grabbed the back of Henri's t-shirt and tugged insistently.

"You'd best do as you're told, girly," the mate said. "Your aunt'll be none too happy if you go overboard and get yourself chewed up by the propeller or caught on the rocks, they're dangerous round here." With that warning given, he turned and walked away.

Edward waited until the three of them were alone again and then he turned to Henri. "Get down," he said in a voice that carried all the authority a fifteen-year-old could muster.

It was the tugging from Elizabeth, not the command from Edward, that finally got Henri down from the railing. She pulled her t-shirt free from Elizabeth's grasp the moment she had done what was wanted of her, though she paid no mind to the wrinkles left in the material.

"How did he know we're going to stay with Aunt Brenda?" she asked.

Edward shrugged. "It's a small community on a small island. I imagine pretty much everyone on the island knows that Aunt Brenda — the relationship was more distant, but they had been told to call her aunt — is having relatives to stay. Most likely she's been telling everyone who will listen since the arrangements were made. I doubt she's had anything interesting to talk about for ages," he said, making it clear that he thought the island and those who lived there were devoid of excitement. "This is going to be the most boring holiday yet." He shook his head in disgust.

Elizabeth and Henri could only nod in reluctant agreement. They were used to boring holidays that saw them shipped off to one distant relative or another, while their parents jetted off to a succession of exotic locations. It happened every summer, just as it did every Easter, and at least every other Christmas, but this promised to be the worst yet.

"At least we haven't got Obnoxious Ollie with us this time," Henri said, determined to find the positive in the situation.

"That's true." Edward brightened at the thought of the absence of their other cousin, Oliver — he was a Graham rather than a Bligh, as he, Elizabeth, and Henri were — known to the rest of them as Obnoxious Ollie because of the way he behaved, who was normally packed off to relatives with the rest of them. That summer, though, Oliver was absent because he had broken his leg, and was being looked after by other relatives who lived closer to home.

There was silence for a short while as the trio watched their home for the next six weeks get closer, then Elizabeth spoke.

"Do you think they're in the air yet?" she asked of her brother. Her eyes went skyward, as though she could see the plane that would be taking their parents to Kenya for a month-long safari.

Edward glanced at his watch before answering. "They should be. Their flight was due to take off an hour ago." His tone was indifferent. He didn't want to think about their parents, who didn't even care enough about them to see them off, choosing instead to get to the airport early and leave it to the housekeeper to make sure they got to the ferry on time. "I don't know why you bother worrying about them, you know they won't worry about us. We'll get a call a week, maybe an email or two, if we can get the internet out here, and they can get it where they are, and they'll have expensive trinkets for us when they get back."

"And they won't ask us anything about what we did, but they'll expect us to sit and listen while they tell us about all the stuff they did, whether it's fun or not," Henri piped up. "If it wasn't for the presents, I wouldn't even pretend to listen." It wasn't that she was shallow or acquisitive, though she realised some people might see her that way, her parents had good taste when it came to buying gifts from the places they visited and she liked what they bought her more often than not.

The same couldn't be said for Edward and Elizabeth's parents, who seemed only to look at the price tag when buying presents.

2

The ferry had been underway for a little over an hour when it finally completed the twenty-one-mile journey to Bligh Island. With deft handling from the small crew, the boat, which to the cousins seemed more like a historical rust-bucket than an operational mode of transport, settled alongside a stone quay of indeterminate age.

The noisy rumble that had shaken the ferry and run up the legs of everyone on board died away slowly, to be replaced by the gentle slapping of water against stone, and the cries of the birds circling overhead.

For a moment that was all that could be heard, then came a flurry of sounds as the ferry crew, all four of them: the captain and his mate, and the engineer and his mate, came up on deck.

Under the supervision of the captain, who bellowed commands as though he was on a much bigger vessel and dealing with a much larger crew, they secured the ferry and ran a gangplank across to the quay. The crew then began bringing out the cargo they were carrying.

Edward dodged around the crew and made his way inside to where his, Elizabeth's, and Henri's luggage had been put. There was too much for him to manage in one trip, even after Henri, who had followed him, took her rucksack and pair of cases — she always travelled light, whereas Elizabeth liked to bring enough clothes to allow for any eventuality — but he picked up what he could.

No sooner had Henri taken up her cases than they were almost knocked out of her hands by one of the ferry's other passengers. He barged past, knocking her off-balance, grabbed a heavy box, which Edward had struggled to move out of the way, and threw it up onto his shoulder as if it were nothing.

Without so much as a hint of an apology, he departed, almost knocking Henri down again.

"Are you alright?" Edward asked.

"Uh-huh." Henri nodded. She put down the case in her left hand so she could rub her right shoulder. "How rude was he?" She pulled her t-shirt out of the way to examine her shoulder, but she was used to cuts, scrapes, and bruises, and was more concerned by the cause than she was by the likelihood of having another bruise.

"Very," Edward said. "Come on, let's get out of here and find Aunt Brenda." There was a definite lack of enthusiasm in his voice for the prospect of meeting a relative he had never even spoken to on the phone, especially one he was expected to spend the summer holidays with.

Edward and Henri made their way out onto the deck and then across the gangplank to the quay, where they set down their burdens. Elizabeth was already there, and Henri stayed with her while Edward returned for the rest of their luggage.

Unlike the rude passenger, the crew stepped aside as he crossed the gangplank back to the ferry, and in just a couple of minutes, he was back with his sister and his cousin. That was time enough, however, for them to have been joined by a short, wiry-looking lady with salt-and-pepper hair.

"You must be Edward," she said, looking him up and down. "I'm Brenda Bligh, you can call me Aunt Brenda, or just Brenda, I don't mind. It's easier than calling me Cousin Brenda, twice removed, or whatever the relationship really is. We have such a confusing family tree, it's far too difficult to figure it out.

"Shall we go? We've got a bit of a drive before we get to the house." Her manner was brisk, as though she was not accustomed to wasting time.

"Don't you live here?" Henri asked, looking to the end of the quay and the white-washed buildings that made up Blighton. They all looked so alike it was hard to tell one from its neighbours. Only the pub, The Baron, was easy to tell apart, due to it being twice the size of any other building that could be seen.

"Lord no," Brenda said with a shake of her head. "There hasn't been a Bligh living in Blighton for forty years, give or take. My cousin, Neil, was the last one. He left the island when he was eighteen to go to America after his parents died. Me and Lloyd, that's your 'Uncle' Lloyd, have a farm inland. Didn't your parents tell you that?"

"They didn't tell us anything about you, or this place, just that we were coming here for the summer," Edward said, having recovered enough from being overwhelmed by 'Aunt' Brenda, who was not at all how he had imagined her to be based on the other relatives he had encountered, to find his voice. "They didn't even tell us how come we have the same name as this island." He was very curious about that and had asked his parents, but they hadn't answered him, which wasn't unusual since they weren't big on explaining things.

Brenda sniffed. "I guess you'll have plenty to learn while you're here if you haven't been told anything." Picking up the two cases nearest to her she set off towards the end of the quay, where a muddy, green Land Rover sat. "You'll want to visit the library and read the family histories, and I'm sure Father Jacobs, he's a historian in his spare time and claims to know everything there is to know about the island, will be more than happy to answer any questions you have. He'll probably want to take you to the castle and give you a tour, so he can show off everything he's learned about the family."

"Castle?" Henri said excitedly. The very idea thrilled her, and she increased her pace to keep up with the older woman, who walked much quicker, despite her legs being only a little longer. "Is it a real castle, like you see in the movies?" She had never been to a castle before, though she had wanted to, and hoped it was a proper medieval castle, with all the old weapons and suits of armour on display. "Would we really be allowed to see it?"

"I'm not sure what you mean by a real castle, but of course you'd be allowed to see it," Brenda said, amused by the young girl's excitement. "I can't imagine anyone trying to stop you, especially since it's yours."

"Ours?" Elizabeth was stunned. "Really? We own a castle?" She knew her extended family owned a lot of property, mostly in the UK, but abroad as well, but she had never heard that they owned a castle. "How?"

Brenda shoved the suitcases she was carrying into the back of the Land Rover and then turned to face the cousins. "It's what they used to call the 'family seat'. It hasn't been lived in since the Second World War, or just after anyway, but it still belongs to the family. It's been ours, or I suppose yours, since it belongs to your side of the family, since it was built in the fourteen-hundreds. If you're interested, you can find out all about it in the library, or you can talk to Father Jacobs."

Once the last of the suitcases had been squeezed into the back, and all four of them had climbed into the Land Rover, Brenda got them moving.

Throughout the journey, Brenda pointed out landmarks and points of interest to her passengers.

"There's the church. That's where you'll find Father Jacobs. I don't suppose any of you are religious, are you?" Synchronised headshaking answered that question. "Not many young people are nowadays," she said with a sigh that could have been disappointment or resignation. "Still, I'm sure you'll want to talk to Father Jacobs about the island and the family history. If you do, that's where you'll find him. Either there or in the pub. He says he goes there to pick up new stories for his history, and to speak to those of his parishioners who are uncomfortable talking to him about their problems in church." She snorted disbelievingly at that, a sound which made Henri, who had been quick to claim the front passenger seat, giggle. "Everyone knows he likes a bit of a drink, though, and he just uses the parishioners as an excuse."

A little further along they came to the library, though it was clear that it hadn't always been that.

"It used to be the school," Brenda said as she pointed it out. "It's actually part of the town hall, not that you can really call Blighton a town, but nobody knows what else to call the place. This part of the building was used for the school, with a small room put aside for the library, but when they decided there wasn't enough children here to keep the school going, they expanded the library to fill the empty space.

"It's quite good, apparently. They even have a computer connected to that internet thingy — that comment produced another giggle from Henri — that you young people are so keen on. I haven't used it myself; I don't have the time for such things, but I've been told you can find out all kinds of things through it."

Henri nodded enthusiastically. "You can find out just about anything on the internet. You could even find your cousin and his family in America, then you could speak to him, and see him at the same time if there's a webcam."

Brenda looked thoughtful at that but didn't say anything more until she came to the next thing she wanted to point out.

Edward, Elizabeth, and Henri soon discovered that the road did not, as it appeared to do, come to a dead-end at the base of the cliff that formed the rear of the small bay in which Blighton had been built. Just as it seemed the road must end, without going anywhere, a gap appeared in the cliff and Brenda steered them up to the top of the cliff. From there she headed inland, away from the lighthouse that watched over the bay.

Henri was fascinated by her surroundings and looked all around her at the countryside they passed through, searching for anything of interest. Edward and Elizabeth were equally curious about where they were going to be staying for the summer, as Henri saw when she glanced into the back of the Land Rover.

The lighthouse passed out of sight too quickly for her to be sure, but Henri thought she saw someone near the top of it. She assumed it was the lighthouse keeper, and wondered if he lived there, or if he lived down in Blighton since it was so close. She also wondered if they would be able to look around the lighthouse. She was as interested in checking it out as she was in checking out the castle, wherever on the island it was.

The notion that her family owned a castle, one she could explore, and whose secrets might be hers to discover, excited her enormously. Adventure and history were two of her favourite things, and she loved the thought of being able to combine them.

After the lighthouse came a succession of distant houses, scattered amongst fields and country that resembled the moors of Devon. Nearly all the houses seemed to be either abandoned or in need of repair, contributing to the air of desertion that seemed to hover over the land.

Despite the air that all the cousins sensed, Brenda assured them that most of the houses they saw were not empty, they were simply owned by people who struggled to keep them up. The old houses, some of them more than two centuries old, were expensive to repair and maintain, she told them, and often needed specialists, who weren't easy to find.

If it hadn't been for the occasional seabird that appeared overheard, the teens could easily have believed they were driving through Dartmoor, rather than across an island less than two dozen miles off the Cornish coast. Not only was the landscape almost identical to that of Dartmoor, but a similar array of animals wandered in and out of view, and occasionally across the narrow road ahead of them.

Sheep and cattle were by far the most numerous of the animals they saw, but not the only ones. There was the occasional horse ambling along the side of the road, a few goats, and at one point they saw a deer, the appearance of which drew a cry of delight from Elizabeth, who didn't usually care much about animals.

Thanks to a horse, which stopped in the middle of the road and showed no interest in getting out of the way, it took twenty-five minutes for them to reach their destination, instead of the fifteen that Brenda said it usually took.

As they looked around the yard in front of the farmhouse, Edward, Elizabeth, and Henri all concluded that this was the worst thing their parents had ever done to them. They had been dumped in the middle of nowhere, almost literally, and were expected to spend six weeks with people they didn't know.

To make matters worse, they had no signal on their phones, which meant they wouldn't be able to contact their friends or access the internet. The lack of a satellite dish on the house, which was antique, if not actually ancient, told them they wouldn't even be able to distract themselves from their situation by watching television.

Henri was the only one of them who wasn't utterly dismayed by the situation, and even she was disheartened.

Like the houses in Blighton, the farmhouse was white-washed, though it had been some time since the white-wash was last applied. The white was now more of a dingey grey, but aside from that, the house was in better shape than most of those they had passed on the way there and was solidly built, as were the shed, pigsty, and chicken coop that formed part of the yard.

While Brenda drove the Land Rover around the house, so she could put it away in the barn, Edward and Henri struggled across the yard with the bags and cases, with Elizabeth trailing along behind them.

They were almost at the door when it swung open to reveal a tall and slightly stooped old man who smiled welcomingly and gestured for them to enter.

Edward had just stepped into the house when a cry from his sister made him drop the cases he was carrying and turn back to the yard. To his surprise, he found Elizabeth, looking distressed and tearful, on the ground, flecks of mud on her face and in her hair, brown stains on her dress, and a chicken pecking at something at her feet.

"What happened?" He hurried back to his sister to help her up.

"I-I don't know," Elizabeth sobbed as she took her brother's hand and allowed herself to be pulled to her feet. "The ch-chicken came out of nowhere. One moment it wasn't there and the next it was. I didn't even see it until I tripped over it, and now I'm all muddy." Her distress was compounded by the fact that Henri found the situation hilarious.

Henri laughed all the harder when Elizabeth made to wipe away her tears and left a thick line of mud across her cheek, like badly applied makeup.

When Brenda returned from putting the Land Rover away, she found Henri doubled up with laughter, Elizabeth shaking and crying and covered in mud, and Edward attempting to comfort his sister. Her husband meanwhile stood in the doorway, his eyes moving from one teen to the next, an expression of bewilderment on his face as he tried to make sense of the situation.

"What happened?" she asked after taking in the scene.

"Babs got out again and tripped the girl up," Lloyd told his wife. "Apparently it upset her. The younger one seems to find it funny."

Brenda's lips twitched, as though she too found the situation funny, but then she got herself under control.

"Now, now, there's no need to be getting yourself so upset," she said in a gentle voice as she patted Elizabeth on the shoulder. "It's just a little mud, nothing to worry about. Come on, let's get you inside and cleaned up. I'll run you a nice hot bath, then you can put on something clean while I make you a cup of tea and put your dress in soak.

"Your brother can take the luggage upstairs, big strong lad like him should be able to cope, and Henrietta...."

"It's Henri, not Henrietta," she said quickly. Being called by the name her parents had stuck her with, the name she disliked so intensely, was enough to cut off Henri's laughter. "Only my parents call me Henrietta."

"Sorry, Henri," Brenda corrected herself. "Would you mind helping your Uncle Lloyd catch Babs and put her back in the coop?"

Henri's eyes went to the chicken, which was still pecking away at whatever it had found on the ground, so she could assess what was being asked of her, and then she said, "Okay," sure it wouldn't be too difficult to catch the bird.

"I hate this place," Elizabeth said as she was guided into the house. "I hate it. I don't know why we had to come here. I wish they'd just let us stay at home with the housekeeper. At least we'd be able to contact our friends and do things then."

"I'm sure once she's cleaned up and has a chance to look around properly, she'll change her mind," Lloyd remarked as he moved to cut off Babs the chicken, whom Henri was chasing around the yard.

Henri wasn't so sure. She suspected it would take something special to make her cousin change her mind about the place. She wasn't surprised by her reaction to what had happened, Elizabeth had never been keen on getting dirty. Henri had known her to change her entire outfit because of a single, barely visible, mark.

Getting dirty wasn't something that bothered Henri, but in one respect she did agree with her cousin. She too would have preferred it if they could have stayed at home, being looked after by their housekeepers, not that they needed much looking after. The thought of spending the summer out of contact with her friends, without even the internet for entertainment, was more than a little depressing.

Henri put Elizabeth from her mind then and concentrated on the job in hand, which was proving more difficult than she had thought it would.

It was ten minutes before Henri finally trudged into the house, where she was shown through to the kitchen by Lloyd, who announced their arrival with the comment, "I don't think we should get her to catch any pigs for us, dear."

Edward looked around from the solid, scarred table that took up half the space in the kitchen and gaped. It was several long moments before he found his voice, and when he did, all he could think of to say was, "What on Earth happened to you?"

Henri grinned broadly, happily, her teeth shining more starkly white than usual against the mud that covered her from head to toe. It was almost impossible to see her face beneath a mud pack that would have cost a small fortune in a top London spa, and only a small patch of blonde showed through the mess she had made of her hair.

"I caught Babs," she said proudly, as though the achievement was worth the mess she had made of herself.

If anyone had told her when she got up that morning that she would catch a chicken before lunchtime, and that she would get covered in mud while doing so, yet still feel pleased with herself, she would not have believed them.

Her initial reaction to the chicken eluding her had been annoyance, but after falling over several times and getting muddy, she had found the fun in the situation.

After looking Henri up and down, Brenda couldn't help but mirror her smile. "I think you're right, if she gets that muddy catching old Babs, I hate to think how bad she'd get if she had to catch one of the pigs." She chuckled as she tried to remember the last time she had seen someone so dirty. "We'd best see if your cousin's finished in the bath, so you can get cleaned up."

"Okay." Henri kicked off her muddy trainers so she wouldn't track any more mud through the house than she already had and followed Brenda from the kitchen.

3

Unhappily dressed in the excessively girly, pastel-pink, pyjamas that had somehow ended up in her luggage in place of the oversized t-shirt and shorts she normally wore to bed, Henri picked up the mug of hot chocolate from the bedside table and crossed to the window.

She twitched the curtain aside so she could look out and peer up at the sky. Used to the light pollution in more populated areas, it surprised her to see the quarter moon shining so brightly, and to see so many stars twinkling in the darkness above.

She was transfixed, and the spell was only broken when Elizabeth entered the room, grumbling, as she had been for most of the day.

"I can't believe I have to share a bed with you." Elizabeth looked in disgust from Henri to the double bed they were both expected to sleep in.

She had been shocked and dismayed when she was shown the bedroom she was to share with Henri and saw there was only one bed for the two of them.

"It's bad enough when I have to share a bedroom with you — that had happened a few times when they were dumped on distant, and less well-off, relatives — without having to share a bed."

Amused, Henri turned away from the window, letting the curtain fall back to block out the starry sky.

"I don't know what you're complaining about, I'm not the one who snores. I'm not the one who wriggles like an eel during the night either."

Elizabeth scowled but didn't respond to that. Instead, she made her way around the bed to the chair in the corner of the room. She nudged Henri's untidy pile of clothes out of the way and set down her own clothes, which were neatly folded and looked as though they had just been ironed. She looked at the bed then, as if to decide which side she was going to sleep on, but there was no decision for her to make for Henri had already claimed the side nearest the window.

Collecting her tablet from her bag, she got into bed and fussily propped the pillows up behind her as she adjusted the covers over her legs. That done, she turned on her tablet and settled down to read, picking up her book where she had left off that morning.

Henri was tempted to ask Elizabeth what she was reading, more to annoy her than out of any real curiosity, but decided against it. Elizabeth was too irritable for it to be fun.

Retrieving her own tablet, she joined her cousin in the bed.

Rather than sit up like Elizabeth, she lay down, her head back on the pillows and her knees up so she could rest her tablet against them and see the screen. She made a brief and futile attempt to access the internet and then settled down to pass the time with a game.

Across the passage from the bedroom Elizabeth and Henri were sharing, Edward lay in the single bed that occupied the second spare room. Her voice had been low, but he had heard his sister's unhappy comments concerning the sleeping arrangements and could understand her annoyance, though that didn't stop him from being amused by the situation.

His amusement didn't last long for his mind turned quickly to the six weeks that lay ahead of them. Six weeks which promised to be filled with boredom.

Edward had long ago accepted that he and his sister were not going to be taken to any of the foreign places their parents visited several times a year. It wasn't fair, but it was a fact of life, as was them, and their two cousins, being either sent to a camp or dumped on whatever relative, no matter how distant, who could be persuaded to take them — he knew well enough that the persuasion usually took the form of a financial incentive.

They were normally able to find something positive about whatever place they were sent to, even if they did generally feel that the holidays were to be endured, rather than enjoyed.

This holiday, it seemed on first day observations, was going to be harder to endure since they were staying on an island that appeared not to have advanced much since the nineteen-fifties.

As far as he could tell, the nearest entertainment was on the mainland, which was only accessible by a ferry that ran just twice a day, first thing in the morning and then again in the evening. Even the nearest internet connection was five miles away, and he had no idea how they could get to it since Brenda and Lloyd had work to do on the farm that would most likely keep them from providing transport.

What they were supposed to do to keep themselves occupied he had no idea.

With his mind tumbling over and over, trying to think of some way to keep himself, his sister, and his cousin occupied during their time on the island, he closed his eyes. It was early to be going to sleep but there was nothing else for him to do, and he hoped that when he woke in the morning the situation would somehow have changed, and things would look better.

4

Edward woke from a deep sleep to the sound of knocking and a strange voice, telling him it was time to get up.

It was several moments before he was awake enough to recognise the voice as that of his only recently met relative, 'Aunt' Brenda, at which point he responded with a call of his own, "I'm awake," though he didn't feel it.

The knocking stopped and Brenda's voice came again. "Breakfast'll be ready in five minutes."

Edward barely had time to acknowledge that and to hear Brenda's footsteps recede, before the bedroom door flew open, and Elizabeth swept into the room.

"Can you believe it," she said in an aggrieved tone. "It's barely half-past six. We're supposed to be on holiday!"

Crossing the room, she dropped onto the bed, her weight across her brother's legs, with an overly dramatic sigh, which was extended when a thin shaft of light found a chink in the curtains and shone directly in her face.

"Can you remember the last time we had to get up at half-past six during a holiday? It's ridiculous."

Edward could remember, but it wasn't he who answered Elizabeth's question. It was Henri who answered as she hopped into the room while trying to pull a sock onto her left foot.

"It was yesterday, we had to get up early to get the ferry over here. We had to get up early at Easter as well, so we could go to Alton Towers, remember? We had to get up at five so we could be there when it opened. Ollie ate too much and got sick, and when he threw up, you threw up too. You must remember that, Lizzie; Ollie threw up all over your favourite dress, that lemon thing you were going on about for ages, and you threw up over your shoes."

The memory of that incident made Henri smile, which contrasted with the angry scowl on Elizabeth's face. It was clear that she didn't want to be reminded of a day that had been deeply embarrassing and upsetting for her.

"You had to buy new clothes from the gift shop and throw away what you were wearing. You were so angry with Ollie you actually hit him."

"I remember," Elizabeth said dully before turning her attention to her brother and asking in a falsely cheerful voice, "So, what are we going to do today?"

"Well, since it seems we're not going to be allowed to sleep in until a reasonable time, I was about to get dressed and go downstairs for breakfast," Edward said. "Brenda and Lloyd didn't say much about what there is to do on the island yesterday, so I think we should get some details after breakfast, so we can decide how we're going to spend the day."

"You think there might be something for us to do?" Elizabeth asked pessimistically.

"Aunt Brenda said I can feed the chickens," Henri said, though whether she intended that Elizabeth should be jealous of her for having something to do or that she should help with the chore wasn't clear. What was clear was that Henri was excited by the prospect, despite, or perhaps because of, the mess she had made of herself while dealing with Babs the day before.

Edward wasn't sure about Henri being involved with animals that possessed sharp beaks. He suspected it was almost a certainty she would get injured in some way, and from experience, he knew he would get the blame, regardless of whether it was his fault or not.

He was about to say something, he didn't know what, when Henri abruptly left the room. To avoid being told she couldn't do what she wanted to, he was sure.

Henri had barely shut the door behind her when Brenda called up the stairs, "Are you lot coming down? Breakfast won't stay hot for long."

"We'll be right there," Edward called back, wriggling his feet as a signal to his sister that he wanted to get up, so he could get dressed.

Brenda, Lloyd, and Henri were already seated at the scarred and well-used table in the kitchen, which was laden with food, when Edward and Elizabeth made it downstairs. Edward was in jeans and a t-shirt, but Elizabeth was still in her pyjamas, which drew a disapproving look from Lloyd, though he made no comment as they joined the rest of them at the table.

"Good morning," Brenda said brightly, ignoring the look on her husband's face. "Did you both sleep alright?"

Edward nodded. "It took me a while to drop off, it's quieter than I'm used to, but once I did, I slept well."

"And you, Elizabeth?" As she asked the question, Brenda began filling two plates from the dishes on the table.

Elizabeth didn't answer straight away, she was too amazed by what she was seeing. She had thought the servings provided the previous day for lunch and dinner had been out of the ordinary, they had certainly been larger than she was used to, but it was obvious that wasn't the case.

Her eyes were huge with shock as she watched Brenda pile a plate with bacon, sausage, tomato, and scrambled egg before setting it in front of her. There was no way she was going to eat a fried breakfast, just the thought of what it would do to her figure and her complexion was enough to make her feel as though she was going to break out in enough spots for her to look like a dot-to-dot puzzle.

"I'm sorry, I can't eat that," she said, pushing the plate away. She looked away from Henri, who was finishing the last of her breakfast as if she hadn't put away a man-sized portion of dinner last night, to her brother, who was eating slowly.

"Are you alright?" Brenda asked in concern, reaching out to lay a hand on Elizabeth's forehead. "You're not coming down with something, are you?"

"I'm fine. I'm just still full after that big dinner yesterday. Besides, I never eat much for breakfast. A bit of fruit is normally enough for me."

Lloyd looked up in surprise. "You'll need more than a bit of fruit to keep you going around here," he said. "It takes a lot of energy to get through a day on a farm. We don't have half as much to do as we did a few years ago, but there's still plenty to keep you busy."

There was silence around the table as what he had said sank in. The only noise to be heard was the clicking of Henri's knife and fork as she finished her breakfast. The silence was only broken when Elizabeth and Edward had shared a long look that was equal parts horror and dismay.

"We're not here to work for you," Edward said. "We're on holiday, and I'm sure our parents have paid you well to look after us for the summer." He didn't know how much their parents had paid Brenda and Lloyd, but he was sure it was a sizeable sum.

"Of course you're not here to work," Brenda said. "You mustn't mind Lloyd, he's old-fashioned, thinks everyone on a farm should share the work." She turned her attention to Elizabeth then. "We don't have much fruit in the house at the moment, but I'll get some in if you tell me what you'd like. Is there anything else I can get you for breakfast?"

"No, thank you, I'll be alright." In the absence of her usual breakfast, Elizabeth made do with a mug of tea, with no sugar, and a lightly buttered slice of toast.

"I should have thought to ask your parents if you have any issues with food." Brenda's voice held a reproving note that was aimed at herself for not having thought of such a possible problem. "You will tell me if there's anything you don't like. I imagine we eat more simply than you're used to, but I'm sure we can cope with any preferences you have."

Elizabeth nodded her thanks, aware that out of her, her brother, and her cousin, she was the one most likely to have a problem with whatever food was served up.

"What are the three of you doing today, if you're not going to help around here?" Lloyd asked once they had all finished eating.

Edward shrugged on behalf of them all. "We haven't made up our minds. We don't know what there is to do around here yet."

The question of what they were going to do with their day wasn't answered until after Henri had helped to feed the chickens and carried the remains of their breakfast out to the pigpen, where it was enjoyed by the sow and her litter.

Once Henri was finished with those chores, which were enough to make her happy, even if they didn't take long, Brenda drove them down to Blighton, while Lloyd got on with the rest of the jobs that had to be done to keep the farm going.

5

In unison, Edward, Elizabeth, and Henri looked up and down the narrow street outside Blighton's small shop, where they had been dropped off. As far as they could see it made no difference which direction they went exploring in for it was all the same, a row of neat, white-washed houses that led to more of the same.

After a brief discussion, they decided to go to their right because the sea was somewhere in that direction.

The few people they encountered were polite, which was something positive to be said for the place, but there was also an air about them that made it clear the cousins were strangers and not truly welcome.

They stopped when they turned a corner a street away from the sea and found the church. Ordinarily, a church would not have been of much interest to them, their family was not a religious one, but the knowledge that their options for entertainment were limited convinced them to go inside and look around.

The huge oak doors, bound in iron, stood open in invitation at the top of a short flight of stairs. It was an invitation they accepted with only minimal reluctance.

The first thing they saw upon entering the church was the large, stained glass window over the altar. Twenty feet high and fifteen feet wide, it depicted the Sermon on the Mount in vivid colours.

For more than a minute they stared at the window without moving, taking in all the details. Only when a lonely cloud drifted in front of the sun and the colours muted did they turn their attention elsewhere.

"It says here that the church is dedicated to Saint Nicholas, the patron saint of sailors," Henri said, reading from a plaque she had found on the wall to one side of the double doors. "It was commissioned in fourteen-thirty-seven by Edward Bligh, first baron of Bligh Island, and completed in fourteen-seventy-one when it was consecrated by the Archbishop of Canterbury, and officially opened by the third baron, Owen Bligh.

"Blimey, it took them a while to build the place." She looked around, gauging the size of the church and then said, "It only took them nine months to build that new housing development outside of town, and that's about twenty times the size of this place."

"I know, but it took longer to build everything in those days," Edward said. "They would have had to get the stone from a long distance away. Even if there was a quarry on the island, it wouldn't have been easy to get the stone from there to here. They built things to last back then as well. Can you imagine the housing development lasting over five hundred years?"

"They certainly did, young man."

The unexpected voice made Edward, Elizabeth, and Henri spin around quickly, their hearts in their throats, to see who had spoken. None of them had heard or seen any sign that there was anyone else in the church with them.

The speaker was the priest, Father Jacobs, whom they had been told about the day before. He was a tall and thin man of middle years, with a thick mop of black hair that was as dark as his priestly robes.

"With a few exceptions," Father Jacobs said as he moved down the central aisle towards the teens, "all the buildings on the island have stood for at least a century, and much longer in many cases." He stopped in front of the trio and looked them up and down. "Would I be right in thinking that you are Edward, Elizabeth, and Henrietta Bligh?" he asked.

"It's Henri, not Henrietta." "How do you know our names?" Henri and Edward spoke at the same time, their words overlapping.

Father Jacobs looked at the offended young girl for a moment, a hint of a smile playing about his lips, as though he found her response amusing, before turning his attention to Edward.

"Your Aunt Brenda told me you were coming to stay with her, she knows I have an interest in the history of the island and the Bligh family, and I took a guess. It's a few days too early for you to be tourists, and we don't get many of them in any case."

Edward was unsurprised to hear that Brenda had told the priest about them coming. He doubted that Brenda and Lloyd had much contact with the family and was sure that Brenda at least was so excited by the visit she had told everyone she spoke to about it.

"Would you like me to show you around?" Father Jacobs asked. "I realise I'm probably not your first choice for a tour guide, but I have studied the history of Bligh Island and your family, and I probably know more about it than anyone. Not only that but I have the key to the crypt. I can take you down to meet your ancestors, the Barons Bligh, if you're interested in that kind of thing."

Henri's face lit up. "That'd be brilliant," she said excitedly, thinking of how jealous her friends would be when they heard about it. She turned to her cousins. "Can we go down?"

Regardless of what Edward and Elizabeth said, she intended visiting the crypt, it was too good an opportunity to pass up. She had never been in a crypt before and didn't know what one was like, but her imagination was active enough to create a mental image that might or might not be close to what lay beneath the church.

Elizabeth wanted to say no and to forbid her cousin to go into a crypt with a man she had only just met, even if he was a priest — quite apart from the dangers she was sure must exist in an underground chamber filled with graves or coffins, or however the barons had been laid to rest, she was sensible enough to know that it was far from a good idea to go anywhere with a stranger — but she saw that her brother was also intrigued by the idea. Since that was the case, she bowed to the inevitable and gave a quick nod of assent.

Father Jacobs was pleased. He got a few people who were interested in being shown around during the tourist season, but not many, and like most historians, he liked nothing more than having someone listen as he revealed the things he had learned about the past. This was better than relating to tourists, though, because the teens were connected, albeit distantly, to that history.

"I guess the best place for me to start," he said after a moment's reflection, which was nothing more than an attempt to inject some drama into what he was about to say, "is with Edward Bligh, the first baron, after whom you are most likely named."

"I'm named after my great-uncle," Edward said. "He died in a boating accident when he was a kid, at least that's what my parents told me."

"I'm sure you are," Father Jacobs said agreeably. "But he was probably named after the first baron. Edward is a name that crops up often in the Bligh family tree, and the first known occurrence is with Edward, Baron Bligh, who was granted the title and lands, namely this island, in fourteen-thirty-four by King Henry VI, in gratitude for services rendered..."

"What did he do?" Henri asked, eager to hear about her family's history. She was sure that even Elizabeth, though she was trying hard not to show it, was delighted to discover that she was descended from a noble family that could be traced back almost six centuries. How they hadn't heard before that they were descended from a baron, she had no idea.

If there was one question Father Jacobs had hoped wouldn't be asked, it was that one.

"I don't know," he admitted unhappily. "I've tried to find out what he did, and I'm sure it must be recorded somewhere, but I've had no luck. What I do know is that the first thing Edward Bligh did was commission his castle, which I don't suppose you've had a chance to see yet, and a series of watchtowers, which were built on the clifftops around the island to watch for invaders. At that time, it was primarily the French they were on the lookout for since we had been in an on-and-off war with them for some time.

"Most of the watchtowers, a dozen were built in total, are gone now, having collapsed or been destroyed over the centuries.

"Unfortunately, Edward Bligh did not live to see either his castle or his church completed. He was killed in a fall from his horse. The records aren't clear, but it seems likely that he suffered some kind of head injury. He was succeeded to the title of Baron Bligh by his son, Henry, who lived to see the castle built, but was killed shortly afterwards, before the church was completed, in a duel over an insult offered to his sister when she refused a suitor."

"He got into a fight and died because someone insulted his sister?" Elizabeth was both appalled and delighted by the idea. She couldn't help looking around at her brother and wondering if he would ever fight someone because they had insulted her. She had a hard time picturing him doing so, he had never been an aggressive or physical sort.

Father Jacobs nodded. "In that era, and even up to the nineteenth century, duels were often fought over honour and insults, especially when a high-born lady was involved.

"Baron Henry was a capable warrior, according to what I've read, but his opponent was better, and in victory, he demanded the Lady Catherine's hand in marriage. I suspect he had his eye on Bligh Island since the suddenly elevated Baron Owen was only fourteen."

"What happened? Did the guy marry Lady Catherine and get the island?" Henri couldn't see how that had happened since the island had obviously remained in the hands of the family.

"No. Baron Owen, grief-stricken by what had happened, challenged Sir Robert. Reports of what happened are sketchy and conflicting, with some saying Owen was a better fighter than his father and he defeated Sir Robert through skill, while others suggest he did so through a combination of luck and Sir Robert having been injured during the first duel. The only thing that is known for certain is that Baron Owen survived, and Sir Robert did not..."

Father Jacobs was long-winded, but it was clear he was knowledgeable, and the cousins lost track of time as they were shown around the church, which included the spot where Baron Owen was interred before the altar.

The history lesson was interrupted abruptly by a voice that boomed from the doorway of the church.

Once Edward, Elizabeth, and Henri had recovered from being startled, they looked around to see that the interruption had come from an overweight constable.

"What was that, Darren?" Father Jacobs asked of the constable, having been so engrossed in his storytelling that he had missed what was said.

"I asked if you've seen that little hooligan, Allen," the constable said, moving further into the church. "I thought I saw him duck in here." He peered around as if he expected to see his quarry appear out of the shadows.

"No, I can't say I have, sorry." Father Jacobs did not sound the least bit apologetic. "Why are you looking for him? What's he been accused of now?"

"That's confidential, Father." The constable made it sound as if he was after Allen for something that was top secret, and of vital importance to national security. "I will say this much, though, he'll be better off if I catch him than if Mrs Leopold does. She's fit to spit and was threatening to tan his hide if she catches up with him." The change in expression on his face suggested he found the thought appealing. "Are you sure he isn't in here? Could he have snuck in while you were somewhere else?"

Father Jacobs shook his head. "I wish I could help you, but I've been here for, blimey, over an hour now." He was surprised to see how much time had passed when he checked his watch. "Along with these three youngsters, Brenda Bligh's relatives. I'm sure you've heard about them coming to stay for the summer. Well, I've been showing them around and telling them a bit about their family, and we haven't seen or heard anyone come in in all that time, have we?"

The cousins all shook their heads, though Henri's eyes strayed from the constable to the confessional, the curtain of which she thought she had seen twitch. When it didn't move again, she decided she must have been mistaken. It didn't seem likely that anyone could have entered the church, let alone made it to the confessional, without being seen or heard by either her, her cousins, or by the priest.

She soon discovered she was wrong.

"If you see him, let me know." With that, the constable turned and hurried from the church.

Father Jacobs waited for about half a minute after the constable left and then he crossed to the confessional. In a quick move, he threw open the curtain that Henri thought she had seen twitch.

Sitting there, an innocent smile on his face, as if he hadn't just been caught hiding from the police, was a boy of about fourteen.

"Well, James, what have you done to upset Mrs Leopold this time," Father Jacobs asked.

"Nothing, Father J, honest," James Allen said immediately, seemingly unconcerned by the lack of belief in the priest's face. "I was just messing about, having a laugh. You know Mrs L, though, she's got no sense of humour."

"Neither has your father," Father Jacobs pointed out, gesturing for James to leave the confessional, which he did without hesitation. "If he hears that you've been bothering Mrs Leopold again and that she's called Constable Lewis about you, well, you know what he'll do."

James nodded. "He'll give me the belt, and he'll probably have me out at the lighthouse with him every day till it's time to go back to school," he said with such obvious distaste that it brought a smile to the priest's lips.

"I'll tell you what I'll do," Father Jacobs said. "I'm running late; I'm supposed to see Mrs Kelly, so if you show Edward, Elizabeth, and Henrietta — sorry, Henri — around, I'll have a word with Mrs Leopold and see if I can get you out of trouble."

James ran his eyes over the cousins, who were watching the exchange with a mixture of curiosity and bemusement, while he decided which was preferable: being in trouble with Mrs Leopold, which also meant being in trouble with his dad, or showing three strangers around. It didn't take him long to come to a decision.

"Sure, I'll show them around."

"Thank you." Father Jacobs smiled in gratitude before turning to the cousins. "I'm sorry to have to cut short my showing you around, but I have to attend to one of my parishioners. If you come back tomorrow morning, I'll finish up the tour and show you around the crypt."

"Can I come too?" James asked eagerly. "I've wanted to look around the crypt for ages, but Father J always says no when I ask him," he said in an aside to the cousins. "You guys must be special if he's willing to take you down there." He cast a mischievous look at the priest as he added, "Unless, of course, he's decided to make you his latest victims. He looks like a nice old priest, doesn't he? Well, he's secretly a devil-worshipper. Every spring and summer he kidnaps a couple of tourists and takes them down to the crypt, where he sacrifices them to try and raise his dark master."

If he was hoping to scare Edward, Elizabeth, and Henri, he was out of luck. All he got for his trouble was looks of derision and a clip round the ear from Father Jacobs.

"Less of your cheek now, or I'll be taking you down to the crypt to make you my sacrifice," Father Jacobs said with a mock threatening look on his face. "And I'll be inviting your father, Mrs Leopold, and Constable Lewis to join me. I'm sure they'd be quite happy to watch you be sacrificed."

"Watch, hell, they'd probably all volunteer to be the one doing the sacrificing."

"Probably," Father Jacobs agreed, his threatening look changing to a smile as he turned his attention to the cousins. "So, how about it? James here will show you around the village and the accessible parts of the island today, and I will finish the tour of the church and the crypt tomorrow." He waited until they had all nodded, with only Henri showing no concern about being placed in the hands of a guide who was barely a year older than her, and whom they had already seen was being sought by the local police, and then he fixed James with a stern look. "Now, don't you be getting them mixed up in any of your usual foolishness, or you'll have me to deal with.

"Don't let him talk you into doing anything stupid or dangerous. He's a good lad, but he hasn't got the sense the good Lord gave a cow." With that warning delivered, he strode away and disappeared through a door at the rear of the church, leaving the four teens alone.

It was a short while before any of them said or did anything. They simply stood there, the cousins on one side of the aisle and James Allen on the other, sizing each other up.

It was Edward who finally broke the silence to say, "Is there a café or somewhere we can get a drink?" He couldn't remember if one had been mentioned yesterday when Brenda was pointing out the places of interest.

James nodded. "Yeah, The Stormy Teacup, I'll show you where it is." He dodged around a row of pews and made for the doorway, stopping when he got there to be sure he was being followed — he was.

6

It didn't take them long to reach the café, which was only a couple of streets from the church. Not that it would have taken them long if it had been on the opposite side of Blighton.

The Stormy Teacup was one street back from the small harbour, but thanks to it being on a corner it had a view of the bay, and the two boats that bobbed up and down there.

A bell rang when they pushed open the door, announcing their arrival and summoning a woman from the back.

James smiled at the woman and whispered to Edward, Elizabeth, and Henri, "That's my aunt. If we're lucky, she'll fix us up with some free cake." He licked his lips in anticipation as he approached the counter. "She makes the best cake." He spoke in a normal tone then, "Hi, Aunt Claire."

"Don't you 'Hi, Aunt Claire' me, James Allen," the woman said, moving around from behind the counter so she stood in front of her nephew, where she could look down on him. "What have you been up to? I've had Constable Lewis in here looking for you, he was threatening to call your father. I had to calm him down with a coffee and a double helping of cake."

"It's nothing," James said quickly, taking a seat at the counter. "I was bored and messing about, just throwing stones at things. Not near anyone or anything breakable," he added hastily. "It wasn't my fault Mrs L's dog got out and was wandering around loose."

"What happened? You didn't hurt the dog, did you?" Claire Allen asked sharply.

James shook his head. "She just got spooked when she almost ran into one of the stones I threw. She ran off, got herself dirty going through a puddle, and got her hair all tangled up when she ran into a bush. It was nothing. She just needed a bath and a bit of a brush, but you know how Mrs L gets. She acts like the yappy little thing is a kid, not a dog.

"Father J said he'd have a word and sort her out."

Claire Allen looked down on her nephew for several long moments as if gauging whether he was telling the truth. Finally, she seemed to decide he was for she gave a satisfied nod and the angry look on her face eased.

"You'd better hope Father Jacobs can calm her down and speak to Constable Lewis before your father hears about this, otherwise you'll be getting the belt when you get home."

James winced in anticipation of the punishment he hoped to avoid. He had been given the belt a few times over the years, when he had been caught doing something wrong, and it was a punishment he wasn't eager to receive again, especially for something that wasn't his fault.

Claire Allen turned her attention, and a welcoming smile, to the trio with her nephew then.

"Hello, and welcome to The Stormy Teacup, the best place on Bligh Island to get yourself a cup of tea and a bit of cake, or something more substantial if you fancy."

"The only place on the island," James said quietly, though not quietly enough. He grinned cheekily when his aunt scowled at him. "Well, you can't really count the café at the castle, it's rubbish. Well, it is, everyone says so. They don't have you baking their cakes, that's why."

"You've got your father's charm, there's no denying that," Claire Allen remarked. "So, tell me who your friends are."

"This is Edward, Elizabeth, and Henri. Her name's Henrietta really, but she doesn't like being called that. They're staying with Mrs B, Mrs Bligh, I mean," James told his aunt before adding, "They're related to the Baron, so they own the whole island. We're all their tenants, so we have to be nice to them."

That came as a surprise to the cousins, who were still struggling with the news that they were related to nobility and owned a castle. It wasn't that they were unused to the notion of their family owning property and having tenants, but it was the first time they had met any of those tenants, and the idea that their family owned an entire island was startling.

"Stop it, James, you're embarrassing them," Claire said. "Welcome to the island. How are you finding it so far?"

"Surprising," Edward said honestly. "Until yesterday, we had no idea one of our relatives is a baron and has a castle, and we didn't know the family owns an island until today." He suspected that if anyone in the family still held the title of Baron Bligh, it was his great-grandfather, whom he had only met twice because he was elderly, bedridden and apparently too senile to recognise most of his family.

"I'm sure it's a good surprise, though," Claire remarked. "Anyway, since this is the first time we've had a member of the baron's family in here, in my lifetime at least, I think the occasion deserves some cake and something to drink. Why don't you all take a seat and have a look at the menu. Pick anything you like, it's on the house."

Edward, Elizabeth, and Henri all protested, assuring James' aunt that they were more than happy to pay for whatever they ordered. Claire insisted that she couldn't possibly charge them, however, especially when she intended, she admitted with a grin, getting a plaque made declaring that the café was frequented by the family of Baron Bligh, and would be adding it to the café's website to encourage business.

THEIR STOMACHS FULL, Edward, Elizabeth, Henri, and their new friend, James, wandered along the harbour front after leaving The Stormy Teacup.

James was in front, as though leading them, but they had no firm destination in mind. He took them from the quay towards the beach, as he described the strip of sand on the far side of the bay in which Blighton had been built.

The harbour came to an end at a wide line of treacherous-looking rocks that reached out into the sea. On the other side of the rocks was the beach, a narrow stretch of multi-coloured sand at the base of the cliff, barely wide enough for the four of them to walk along side-by-side.

"I know it doesn't look like much of a beach," James said as their feet sank into the strange mix of white, gold, and black sand. "I'm sure you're all used to much better beaches. Big ones with sand all one colour, water you can swim in, and nice, hot sun." He tried hard not to sound jealous. "It's all we've got, though. At least, it's all we can get to. There's another bit of a beach at the bottom of the cliff below the castle, but you can't get to it except by boat, and it's not worth bothering with even then."

Henri snorted. "Our parents go to places that have those kinds of beaches, but they don't take us. We always get dumped on relatives during the holidays. Mostly the beaches we've been to have been British, though I have been to France a couple of times. Not that the beaches I went to there any different to the ones in Britain."

Edward and Elizabeth said nothing. They hadn't been as lucky as James thought they had been, but they had visited a few beaches that matched his description before their parents decided they preferred to holiday without their children.

They walked on in silence for a while, continuing to the end of the beach, which didn't take them long for it was less than half a mile long.

When the sand finished, James led them over to the cliff face.

Bemused, the cousins watched as James began to feel around the dark rock just a few feet from where the sea lapped at the sand.

When James' strange behaviour continued for more than a minute,

Elizabeth felt compelled to ask, "What are you doing?" It seemed to her that he was looking for something, but she couldn't imagine what, since the only thing she could see was the dark rock of the cliff face.

James turned away from the cliff for a moment to smile and say, "It's a surprise." He found what he was after a few moments later. "And here it is." He looked around, expecting to see excitement or at least interest, but all he saw was bemusement and bewilderment. Fortunately, he knew a way to fix that.

He moved until he was right up against the cliff face, paused for a moment, and then took a step forward, at which point he vanished. One moment he was on the narrow beach with the cousins, and the next he was gone.

Edward, Elizabeth, and Henri all gasped. They looked around, trying to work out how James could have disappeared so suddenly and so completely that he appeared to have melted into the cliff.

Magic was the only answer they could come up with, and that was quickly dismissed. They were all smart enough to know that magic was just an illusion, and there hadn't been time for James to set up any kind of trickery to fool them with.

James listened to his new friends trying to work out what had happened to him for almost a minute before he decided it was time to reappear.

Edward and Elizabeth, being older, tried to conceal their amazement, despite the fuss they had made just a few moments ago. Henri had no problem revealing what she was thinking and feeling, however.

"How did you disappear like that?" she wanted to know. "Where did you go?" She examined the face of the cliff where James had disappeared and reappeared for a third time but could see no sign of how he had accomplished the trick.

James grinned as he said. "Magic." He let that hang in the air for a moment, even though he could see that none of them believed him, and then he told them. "There's an opening. It's almost impossible to see, even when you're right in front of it, that's why I had to feel around for it. It goes back into the cliff before opening out into a small cave, and there's a tunnel that leads all the way to the top of the cliff. It comes out near one of the watchtowers, one of the ones that collapsed years ago.

"You wanna see it?" he asked. He hadn't planned on showing them the tunnel when he took them to the beach. It was his secret, somewhere he liked to come and mess about, or just to be on his own, but seeing the looks of surprise his disappearing trick had generated he wanted to surprise them some more, and to show off a little.

Henri nodded, matching her new friend's eagerness with her own. "Yeah. Come on, let's go exploring," she said, turning to her cousins to encourage them.

Elizabeth looked to her brother for a way out. It wasn't that she was afraid of the dark, or of wandering around the inside of a cliff — at least that was what she told herself — but it wasn't very sensible. They would be risking injury, not to mention damage to their clothes, and she didn't fancy that, especially since she was, as she had been yesterday when she was tripped by Babs the chicken, only wearing a thin summer dress.

She was far more vulnerable than her brother and her cousin, both of whom were wearing jeans.

Ordinarily, Edward would have responded to the appeal in his sister's eyes, but he couldn't bring himself to ignore the opportunity to explore. He knew it was partly because he didn't want to look scared or timid in front of the younger teens, and that was silly, but he couldn't help it. He pushed that thought aside and focused instead on the fact that he did quite like the idea of exploring a tunnel that led through a cliff to a ruined watchtower.

"We were after something to do," he said, "and this seems more interesting than anything else we could do."

James grinned, pleased that he was going to have an opportunity to show off his secret. "Let's go, it's through here." He stepped aside so he could show them where the narrow crevice was.

Even being shown where to look, it was almost impossible for the cousins to see the opening. They had to feel around for it.

Once they found the opening, Henri, ever daring and eager for excitement and adventure, entered first, with Edward just behind her. Elizabeth followed, unwilling to be left behind, especially when she didn't know how long they would be gone, but only after a lengthy period of hesitation.

Entering the cliff last, James squeezed past the cousins so he could lead the way.

The short tunnel to the cave was dark, requiring them to grope their way along to avoid bumping into the walls and injuring themselves. Fortunately, there was light when they reached the cave.

The light, which came from a small opening high up in the wall of the cave, was barely enough for them to make out one another's outlines, but it enabled them to see that there was a pool of water a short distance from their feet and avoid it.

If they had gone any further before stopping, they would have ended up with wet feet, or perhaps even drowning since it was impossible to tell how deep the water in the pool was.

Unlike the cousins, James was prepared for the limited light, and from a convenient, waist-high, shelf of rock he took the torch he had 'borrowed' from his father. The torch wasn't very powerful, but it did provide enough light for them to see one another and their surroundings more clearly.

A narrow path ran around the pool of water, which was only about six feet wide, to another tunnel on the other side of the small cave.

"How deep is it?" Elizabeth asked nervously, looking down at the dark pool.

"No idea," James admitted. "I tried measuring it using a stone and some string, but couldn't find the bottom, so I know it's more than twenty feet deep. I'm pretty sure it connects to the sea, it seems to get higher and lower with the tides, and I know what happens to people caught by the tide in the wrong place, so I'm not about to go in there to try and find the bottom."

"How did you find this place?" Henri asked. Given how difficult it had been to find the opening, she doubted he had just stumbled across it, though she soon learned that that was just what had happened.

"I was exploring the top of the cliff near the old watchtower and fell down a hole," James said. "I was able to climb out, fortunately, otherwise I could have been in big trouble, but I saw a tunnel leading somewhere, so after I recovered, I decided to explore and see where it went. There's been rumours about smugglers, and possibly even pirates, using this island over the centuries — Father J says the rumours about pirates is rubbish, he's never found anything about pirates in all his research, but the stuff about smugglers is true — and I wondered if the tunnel had anything to do with them.

"I never found anything to do with smugglers." He looked disappointed. "But I did manage to find my way down to the beach. There's a lot of dead-ends, and some caves, but mostly it's just a way for me to get from the top of the cliff to the beach, or from the beach to the top of the cliff. And it's a good place for me to hide from Constable Lewis when he's after me."

"You had smugglers here?" Henri's eyes shone brightly. She was more interested in that part of James' story than in how he had found the tunnel and the cave. Pirates would be better — she knew that real pirates were hardly at all like they were shown in films and TV shows and in real life pirates rarely buried their treasure because they were too busy spending it, but they were still interesting — but smugglers were almost as good.

"Yes." James nodded. "It was in the seventeen and eighteen-hundreds, so Father J says. They smuggled rum, tobacco, and probably anything else they could make money off. The cliffs all around the island are filled with caves and tunnels, which is probably why they chose this place. I've looked all over for the caves the smugglers are supposed to have used, but I've never found them." He looked unhappy at his failure. "I know where on the island they're supposed to be, but it's really difficult to get to." He dismissed the topic of smugglers then and said, "Come on, we'd better get moving if we're going to make it to the top."

James led the way around the pool, lighting the ground in front of him with his torch. Henri followed on his heels, fearless and eager to explore. Elizabeth went next at Edward's urging, her eyes on the ground at her feet to be sure she didn't slip and fall into the pool, and Edward brought up the rear.

Edward was so intent on making sure his sister and Henri were safe that he didn't realise he was straying himself until he put his foot in the water at the edge of the pool, soaking him to the ankle and making him shiver.

7

A check of his watch upon their return to the outside world revealed to Edward that it had taken them almost ninety minutes to make it from the beach to the top of the cliff.

It was only half a mile in a straight line by his estimation, but he was sure they had travelled several times that while traversing the tunnels that snaked back-and-forth through the cliff.

They might have made better time if they hadn't had to move slowly to avoid the dangers that potentially lurked just outside the light from James' torch. Edward didn't know about the others, but he had imagined there being unknown creatures hiding in the darkness, waiting to pounce at the first opportunity.

Aside from his fanciful imaginings, James had warned of areas where the roof lowered and the unwary might hit their head, and other spots where rocks stuck out from the floor or the sides of the tunnel.

"What do you think?" James asked as he pushed the torch into his pocket and looked around at the cousins.

He could see that Elizabeth hadn't enjoyed the journey through the cliff, but that didn't surprise him. He could have guessed at that before they started. He was sure Edward and Henri had enjoyed it, though, Henri especially. The look on the younger girl's face told him that she felt the same way about the tunnels as he did and that she was indifferent to the scrapes and bruises she had acquired.

"Great," Henri said. "Do the tunnels go anywhere else?" She was eager to go back down and explore, rather than simply following a route from the beach to the clifftop.

"No idea," James admitted. "I haven't explored it all. It's not really safe on my own, and there isn't anyone around here I'd want to show the tunnels to. Most of the ones I have explored are dead ends that go nowhere, though some do end in caves. Not that there's anything exciting about them. There's some tunnels I haven't explored all the way because I don't want to get lost, and they go for quite a distance.

"What about you two?" he asked of Edward and Elizabeth.

"I prefer it out here," Elizabeth said. Unlike her cousin, she was not indifferent to her injuries. Her dress had afforded her little protection from the dangers of the tunnels and was now torn in several places, especially over her left knee, which was a bloody mess. Her knee was by far the worst of her injuries, as proved by the limp it gave her, but she also had scraped and bloody hands, a scratch running down her right shoulder, and a sizeable bruise that covered most of her left shin.

"Are you alright?" Edward asked in concern. He had seen Elizabeth take a tumble on their way through the tunnels and limp afterwards, but he had thought she had twisted her ankle, not hurt her knee.

"I'll be fine," Elizabeth said bravely, wincing as her brother gently wiped at the blood and dirt on her knee with the mostly clean handkerchief he took from his pocket. The pain was almost enough to distract her from the itching in her palms, which she was sure were embedded with little stones she longed to dig out. "Can we go back to the farm, though?" she asked. "I think I've had enough *fun* for one day." The emphasis she put on the word fun revealed how she felt about what they had done that day.

Edward glanced at Henri, who he could see wanted to continue exploring and then back at his sister's knee and nodded. "Sure, we can go back." He ignored the disappointment on both Henri's and James' faces. "I can't get a signal up here, though, so I can't call Brenda."

Henri and Elizabeth both checked their phones and discovered that they too had no signal. Bligh Island, as far as they could tell, was the land forgotten by mobile technology. It was barely twenty miles from the mainland, yet it seemed to receive virtually no mobile phone or internet signal.

For teens used to being able to access the internet or contact their friends whenever they wanted, it was like finding themselves thrown back in time several decades.

"We'll have to get down to Blighton and see if we can get a signal there," Edward said. "Will you be alright to get there?"

"As long as we don't have to go back through the tunnels." Elizabeth shot an unhappy look at the hole in the ground, out of which they had climbed.

James looked downcast at the thought that their adventures were over for the day, but he brightened at Elizabeth's comment. "No, we don't need to go back through them," he said, with what he hoped was a reassuring smile, before adding, "There's a much quicker way down on the other side of the watchtower. It's a little steep, but safe enough."

"Is there another way down?" Edward asked. He worried that his sister might not be able to cope on a steep path with her injured knee, which might lead to her hurting herself again, perhaps more seriously.

James nodded. "There's three ways down from here: back through the tunnels, down the cliff path, or you can follow the road. The road is the safest way, but it's also the longest from here since it's about a mile from here to the road, and then another half a mile or so down to Blighton. The cliff path is the quickest way back down, it shouldn't take much more than half an hour, even with Elizabeth limping, but if you don't like heights, it's not much fun. It's quite narrow and you can see all the way down to the beach and Blighton.

"The tunnels aren't the quickest route or the safest, but if you've got a problem with heights, it's probably the best way down."

He watched the cousins for any sign of squeamishness and was disappointed to see that neither Edward, Elizabeth, nor Henri showed any sign of being disturbed by his description of the cliff path.

"Think you can manage the quick route?" Edward asked of Elizabeth after considering the options for a moment. He wasn't sure how well his sister was going to cope with the cliff path, he preferred the thought of the longer and safer route back to Blighton, but he suspected Elizabeth's leg wouldn't manage the distance.

Elizabeth nodded, though she didn't look convinced as she said, "Yes."

"Okay, we'll take the cliff path."

8

E dward, Elizabeth, and Henri were at a table by the window with James, finishing up their drinks when Brenda pulled up outside in her Land Rover.

"Is everything alright?" Brenda asked when she joined the teens at the table. "I thought it would be at least a couple more hours before you wanted collecting. And seeing how you seem to have made a friend," her gaze came to rest on James, without revealing what she thought of that friend, "I would have expected you to be less keen to be collected."

"I hurt my knee," Elizabeth said, sticking her leg out from under the table to show her injury.

"It's alright, I patched her up," Claire Allen said, coming out from behind the counter. "It looks worse than it is. She'll probably have a limp for a few days, but nothing worse than that, and her hands should heal up in the same time."

Brenda looked alarmed and reached out to take Elizabeth's left hand, which, like her knee, was covered by a large plaster. "What happened?" She wasn't sure what concerned her more, that Elizabeth had hurt herself, or that she had done so on only her second day there, having already taken a fall that left her covered in mud on the first day.

She could only imagine what might happen before the end of the cousins' stay given how the holidays had started.

"We were exploring. James was showing us around and I slipped and fell."

"What about you, Henri?" Brenda asked, having spotted that Elizabeth was not the only one of her charges to have been injured.

Henri shrugged and said, "Lizzie bumped into me when she fell over, and I caught myself on the rocks. We were walking by the beach," she clarified when Brenda looked as though she was about to ask, 'what rocks?'.

Brenda had enough experience with children, though hers were grown and had long ago moved away, to realise that she wasn't being told the truth, at least not all of it. That didn't surprise her, however, since James Allen was involved.

Fortunately, she knew James well enough, as she knew pretty much everyone on the island, to know that he wouldn't have got her charges into any serious trouble. Besides which, she figured that Edward and Elizabeth were sensible enough to avoid trouble even if James had tried to get them into any.

Ordinarily, she would have tried to find out what the cousins had really been up to, as she would have if they had been her children. Just then, though, she figured it was better simply to be pleased that they had made a friend on the island, so they had someone to pass the holidays with.

"How about you?" she asked, turning to Edward. "Did you get hurt when your sister fell over?"

Edward shook his head. "No, I was behind her, so I'm okay."

"Okay, well, thank you for taking care of them, Claire, and thank you for showing them around, James."

James grinned. "No problem, Mrs B. I'll see you tomorrow morning," he said to the cousins. "Remember, Father J said he'd show us around the crypt and finish his tour of the church. After that, there's a few places I can show you."

"We'll be here," Henri assured him, hoping that wherever he intended showing them would prove as fun as the journey through the tunnels in the cliff had been. At no point had they faced danger in the tunnels, despite the injuries they had collected, but it had been exciting all the same, more exciting than anything else she could remember doing. Why that should be, she didn't know, but she wanted to do something similar again, though with a better torch, so she could see things easier. "Can we check out the watchtower tomorrow? I really want to get a better look at that."

With one eye on Brenda, as though he expected her to veto the idea, James nodded. "Sure, we can go there in the afternoon." He got to his feet as the others did and followed them outside. "I'll meet you here at nine."

Edward, Elizabeth, and Henri were all quiet during the drive back to the farm, each of them for different reasons.

Henri was thinking back over the fun she had had, after expecting to be bored, and was looking forward to tomorrow, when she hoped they would have more caves or tunnels to explore or something with the same level of excitement.

Elizabeth was concerned with the possibility that she was going to end up with an ugly scar on her knee that would be visible whenever she wore a skirt or dress.

Edward wasn't thinking about excitement or injuries, he was wondering if Brenda had seen through the story they had agreed on since James didn't want his secret playground revealed, and what she would do if she had.

The moment they reached the farm and Brenda had put the Land Rover away, she took her charges through to the kitchen, where she had them sit down at the table. She then fetched the first-aid kit and, over their protests, the loudest of which came from Henri, proceeded to check them over and treat their injuries, even though Claire Allen had already done so.

Soon enough they were all wincing from the sting of iodine on scrapes and cuts, even Edward who, as the only boy, tried to show that he was tough and could handle the treatment better than his sister and his cousin.

"There you are," Brenda said when she was done. "None of you are hurt bad, that's a blessing, and I doubt this collection of cuts will stop you doing whatever is it you are planning on doing tomorrow. You'll have to be careful, though, Elizabeth. You'll have a limp for a few days like Claire said, but as long as you don't make it worse, you should be alright after that."

"DO YOU REALLY THINK there were pirates and smugglers here?" Henri asked. She was in bed, her tablet forgotten on her lap.

Elizabeth thought about the question for a few moments while she sipped at the hot chocolate Brenda had brought up before answering.

"I don't know. I guess there could have been. James certainly seemed to think so, at least about the smugglers. Maybe we can ask Father Jacobs about it tomorrow. Brenda said he knows the history of the island, so if anyone knows about smugglers or pirates, it's going to be him."

"I think there were," Henri said, making up her mind. She preferred the excitement of there having been smugglers on the island to the alternative. "I wonder if we can find those caves the smugglers used that James mentioned."

Elizabeth smiled briefly, amused by her cousin's enthusiasm. "Don't you think after what happened today," she pointed to her knee, and to the scrapes Henri had picked up, "that it would be dangerous to go exploring more tunnels, especially since if you do find them, James won't know his way through them. You could get hurt, lost, stuck, anything."

"That's what makes it fun," Henri said. "Besides, think what we could find, what the smugglers or pirates might have left behind. Maybe we could find some treasure." That thought excited her and she grabbed her tablet in the hope of finding that she had an internet connection, so she could see if there was anything about pirates or smugglers on Bligh Island for her to read.

To her amazement, she found that she did have a signal, though it was weak, and it took ages for every web page to load. She quickly became frustrated and gave up, turning her mind instead to thinking of a way to get a signal she could use.

Unfortunately, she suspected there was no decent Wi-Fi signal to be had on the island, and the only way for her to access the internet reliably was to get the ferry to the mainland.

9

"Where's Elizabeth?" James asked the moment he joined Edward and Henri at the table by the window of The Stormy Teacup.

"She's decided to stay at the farm today," Edward said. "Her knee was really painful and stiff when she got up and she didn't want to walk on it. Plus, her hands were pretty sore."

"And she wasn't too keen on walking around the crypt. She thinks it'll be scary." When Edward threw her an annoyed look, Henri said defensively, "That's what she said this morning when she was getting dressed. I'm not surprised, are you? Even Ollie's more adventurous than Lizzie. I love Lizzie, you know that, but give her a choice between going exploring, especially somewhere like a cave or a crypt, or doing something safe and boring..."

Edward had to agree. "She'll take safe and boring every time. Shall we go?" he asked of James, who had shown no inclination towards taking a seat.

"Sure. I'm ready if you are."

The doors of the church stood open in invitation when they got there, as they had yesterday, but unlike yesterday, there was someone there. A middle-aged man was seated on a pew at the front of the church, his head bowed in either prayer or thought. Father Jacobs, however, was nowhere to be seen.

"I'll see if I can find Father J," James said, striding away down the aisle to search for the priest, while Edward and Henri slowly moved further into the church without saying anything. Neither of them wanted to disturb the church's other occupant.

Edward and Henri were left to wander around for almost five

minutes before James returned, having disappeared through a door to one side of the building.

"He'll be with us shortly," James said when he reached the cousins, who had both been surprised by the boldness with which James had entered what they assumed was the vestry.

Neither of them was religious, but both Edward and Henri knew that it wasn't usual for a person to just walk into the vestry, which was considered a private area for the priest and other servants of the church.

"He's just taking care of some business." James thought of something then and uttered a quick, and inappropriate given his location, curse. "Have either of you got a torch? I forgot to bring mine, and it's likely to be dark down in the crypt."

"No." Edward shook his head. "I was going to ask Lloyd or Brenda if they had a torch we could borrow but I forgot, what with Elizabeth deciding not to come. I'm sure it'll be okay. I doubt Father Jacobs would have offered to take us down to the crypt if we wouldn't be able to see anything."

Father Jacobs appeared after a minute, closing the door behind him with a hollow bang that echoed through the church. He paused to speak to the man praying in the front pew, and then made his way down the aisle to where the trio of teens waited.

"Good morning, Edward, Henri," he greeted the cousins with a warm smile. "Where's Elizabeth? Is she alright?"

"She's fine," Edward said. "She took a bit of a tumble yesterday and hurt her knee, so she's resting it."

"Well, I'm sure your aunt is taking good care of her. Now, I believe you are here to finish the tour of the church, and to hear the rest of your family's history, as I know it at least."

"And to be shown around the crypt," James said quickly, determined that the part he was most looking forward to wouldn't be forgotten.

"Yes, of course, and the crypt." Father Jacobs favoured James with an amused smile. "Perhaps, since Mr Carrow is attending to his devotions, we should finish the tour and the history first, then I can get my torch and show you all the crypt. Is that okay with you three?"

Edward, Henri, and James all nodded, though Henri, like James, was more interested in the promised trip down to the crypt than the history lesson. She intended taking as many photographs as her phone would hold, so she could show her friends when she went back to school. She wanted to be able to prove that she was descended from nobility, which she was sure would annoy a few of the girls she knew.

Despite her eagerness to see where her ancestors were interred, Henri soon found herself caught up in the history of her family. There were far more barons who had done nothing of import than there were those whose deeds had been deemed worthy of special note, nonetheless the history of the barons Bligh was interesting.

In a passionate voice, which spoke eloquently of his love for the subject, Father Jacobs told of the Blighs, both legitimate and otherwise, who had fought in the first and second world wars, the Peninsula War — the Napoleonic War, to give it its more common name, he explained — and those who had fought in various other military campaigns that Britain had waged over the years.

Aside from their military heritage, which had netted the family numerous medals and commendations, not to mention titles and privileges, over the centuries, many of which could be seen on display at the castle, the Blighs had been involved with many historical events. They were never centre stage, but they had managed to be influential from the sidelines.

"What about pirates or smugglers?" Henri asked once the tour and the history lessons were over, and they were ready to go down to the crypt.

The question, coming as it did when he was in the act of unlocking the door to the crypt, left Father Jacobs bewildered. Pirates and smugglers had not come up at any point during his history lessons, and he couldn't think why they should have.

"What about pirates and smugglers?" he asked.

"James said they used to use this island." Henri's gaze went to her new friend. "Is that true? Were there pirates and smugglers here?"

Father Jacobs was silent for a few moments as he considered how to answer the question.

Finally, he said, "There were smugglers here. They used the island in the seventeen and eighteen-hundreds to smuggle tobacco, silk, rum, and anything else the excise people wanted to impose a duty on. They operated for quite a few years, using a series of caves and tunnels only they knew how to access, with the pub here in Blighton and another on the mainland as covers.

"The ringleader, Solomon Kierney, built a house on the island, it's about a mile from your aunt and uncle's farm, and rumour has it he built it over the clifftop entrance to the tunnels."

"Is that true?" Edward wasn't quite as interested in the story as Henri and James were, but he was intrigued enough to want to hear what Father Jacobs knew.

Father Jacobs could only shrug. "Who can say. Despite all my research and the extensive search that was made of the house by the excise officers after they broke up the smuggling ring, there is nothing to support the rumours. I even searched the property myself but found nothing.

"Of course, by the time I heard the stories and visited the place to make my search it had been a ruin for a century and a half. If the entrance to the tunnels ever was there, it's most likely been destroyed."

"If it's there, I'll find it," James said determinedly.

Father Jacobs smiled and ruffled his hair. "If God wishes those tunnels to be found, I'm sure you're just the scamp he'll let find them." He unlocked the door in front of him and then tucked the large, iron key safely back into his pocket.

Henri wasn't satisfied with the answer she had been given, and as

she descended the rough stone stairs by the light of the torch in Father
Jacobs hand, she said, "What about pirates? There were smugglers here,
what about the pirates James mentioned?"

Father Jacobs was amused by how much the young girl reminded
him of himself. When he got a question in his mind, he wasn't satisfied
until he had as full an answer as it was possible to get. He was sorry he
had to disappoint her.

"To the best of my knowledge, no pirates sailed from this island,
hid treasure here, or retired here in luxury after giving up their life of
plunder and pillage. I know James dreams of one day discovering buried
pirate treasure and becoming rich."

James flushed in the torchlight. He hadn't realised that his secret
desire was known to anyone, least of all the priest.

"But I've never found any evidence of any on the island," Father
Jacobs said. "Of course, that doesn't mean there isn't a connection
between the island and piracy. In seventeen-twenty-two, the third son
of Baron Franklin, Edgar, decided he didn't want to go along with the
marriage plans his father had for him — he was to marry a reportedly
unattractive daughter of a lord with good lands, a solid fortune, and no
heir — so he ran away and joined the navy. He then ran away from the
navy when he got into trouble and joined a pirate crew."

"What happened to him?" Henri asked excitedly, thrilled by the
thought that one of her ancestors had been a pirate, or at least the
relative of one had been.

"I have no idea," Father Jacobs admitted. "The last I was able to
find on him was an order from the Royal Navy, declaring that he had
been found guilty in absentia of striking an officer, theft, desertion, and
piracy, and was sentenced to be hanged, with the sentence to be carried
out by any agent of His Majesty's government who should encounter
him. I haven't found anything to suggest that Edgar Bligh was ever
caught, though, let alone hanged for his crimes."

The tour of the crypt didn't take long, and in the eyes of the three teens, it was both exciting and a disappointment. It was exciting because of what it was, a dark crypt that held the bodies of more than five centuries worth of the barons Bligh, more than five hundred years of history.

The disappointment came from the fact that there wasn't much to see. Each baron had been laid to rest in a stone sarcophagus that bore a carved likeness of the man interred within, and a brief inscription describing their life. Some likenesses had worn away to the point where it was hard to tell they had once been a face, while others, the more recent ones, were still visible.

The sarcophagi were similar enough that only a true historian would have taken the time to examine them all, and the teens were soon bored of them.

10

B arely half an hour after descending into the darkness of the crypt, Edward, Henri, and James walked out of the church and into the late-morning sunshine.

A chill had seeped into the bones of all three while they were amongst the dead. A chill that made them feel as though they had had an encounter with a ghost. They were glad to be back in the sun, even if it did take a while for them to warm up.

While the sun chased the cold from their bones and muscles, they wandered the waterfront. It wasn't a long walk from one end of the harbour to the other and they had to go up and down several times before they felt properly warm again.

"Let's get ice-creams," Henri suggested as they once more reached the end of the quay and paused to watch the gulls that were circling the lone fishing boat in the harbour in the hopes of getting an easy meal. "We can eat them on the way to the watchtower. You said you'd show us it today," she reminded James in case he had forgotten.

James nodded. He hadn't forgotten what he had said, and he had no problem with going to the ruins of the watchtower. He had been there lots of times, but he was sure that, as with his journey through the cliff, it would be more fun with someone to share the experience.

He did, however, have a problem with getting an ice cream. Not because he had anything against ice cream, he loved it, and was always in the mood for one when the sun was out, but because he didn't have much money. He had to earn every penny he had through chores, and what money he earned had to last him as long as possible.

He didn't want his new friends to think he was poor, though, especially when they clearly had plenty of money, so he said, "Sure, I could go for an ice cream."

"We've only just warmed up," Edward protested half-heartedly before following Henri as she led the way to the shop.

Edward's legs were longer than hers, but such was Henri's eagerness for an ice cream that she reached the shop ahead of him. Unfortunately, that eagerness meant she was perfectly placed to be knocked off her feet when the man who had bumped into her on the ferry yanked open the door and strode out.

He walked straight into her, sending her to the ground with a thump, and carried on as though utterly unaware of what he had done. He didn't even respond when James called him a few choice names.

Edward might have joined James in his name-calling had he not been busy helping Henri to her feet and making sure she was alright. She had suffered nothing worse than having had the wind knocked out of her, thankfully, and once she recovered, she had to be restrained from giving chase so she could repay the man for knocking her down with a kick or a punch, or even just the contents of her mind.

"Who was that guy?" Edward asked once Henri finally calmed down and allowed herself to be led into the shop. He couldn't help thinking that after how the first two encounters had gone, and the guy's apparent indifference to knocking girls down, a third encounter was likely to lead to Henri being hurt.

"Patricks, Sean Patricks," James said in a voice that expressed his dislike as eloquently as the look on his face. "He's not one of us, not an islander. He wasn't born here, isn't related to anyone from the island, and doesn't even know anyone on the island, at least not as far as I know. He moved here last year, bought some land and built himself a house. He's supposed to have made a fortune selling some company he built up and has retired here. You wouldn't think he was rich to look at him, would you.

"That's about all anyone knows about him. Anyone I know anyway. That and he has a brother who lives on the mainland. I've seen him a couple of times. He's just as unpleasant."

A sniff of disapproval drew the attention of Edward, James, and Henri away from the ice-cream freezer and to the counter. The old lady who stood at the till gave another sniff and pressed her lips tight as though to stop herself speaking. It didn't work, the words she was attempting to suppress burst from her anyway.

"That man is the rudest person I've ever met," she said. "He has no respect for a person's age, sex, or position. If I didn't need the business..." She closed her lips firmly on whatever else she had been about to say. "What can I do for you kids?" she asked after a moment.

"She's a fine one to talk about rude people," James said once they were out of the shop with their ice-creams. "She's as rude as they come. You should hear her when she catches someone reading a magazine in the shop." He shook his head as he recalled the last time he had dared to flick through a magazine to try to decide whether to spend his hard-earned money on it.

IGNORING THE WARNINGS that Edward called out to her, Henri climbed over and around the remains of the watchtower. She gave no thought to the danger she was in as she explored the ruins.

The ground level and the steps leading up to the first level were still largely intact, while the rest had collapsed as a result of some long-forgotten event and lay mostly on the ground, surrounding what was left of the tower, with some of it scattered over and blocking much of the first level.

His heart in his mouth, Edward watched Henri and James as they moved up from the ground level. He had been okay with them coming to the tower, but he hadn't got a good look at the state the place was in the day before, his attention being focused on his sister and her injuries.

Now that he saw the full extent of the damage the historic structure had sustained, he wished they hadn't come. He couldn't help thinking that if he didn't do something, it was only a matter of time before either Henri or James got hurt.

"Come on, Henri, you have to come down from there," Edward called out, trying once again to avert the disaster he could sense was looming. "You're going to fall and hurt yourself if you carry on like that."

"No, I'm not," Henri called back, pausing in her squirrel-like scampering to balance on what had once been a significant portion of the watchtower's battlements to look down on her cousin, who had a worried look on his face. "I'm fine up here." As if to prove her point, she hopped from one foot to the other, her arms stretched out to either side of her for balance, and then jumped onto the next segment of fallen and weather-worn masonry.

Edward felt his heart leap into his throat as he watched Henri. It lodged there and then tried to beat its way out when she landed and the stone under her shifted, making her wobble. She recovered her balance quickly, but that did little to ease his concerns.

It required no effort for him to imagine what would have happened if she hadn't kept her footing. She would almost certainly have been seriously injured, if not killed, as she fell a dozen or so feet and landed on broken masonry.

He shivered, chilled by a cold that was more intense than what he had experienced in the crypt. He rubbed his arms briskly to rid them of the goosebumps that had risen.

The wobble, minor though it was, woke Henri to the danger she was putting herself in. There was a thrill to it, it made her heart drum excitedly in her chest, but she had enough sense to realise that there was no reward to the risk she was taking, and therefore no reason to take it.

From the pile of masonry that had almost made her fall, she hopped down onto more solid stonework, she then turned to James and said accusingly, "There's nothing here," as if he was responsible for her being unable to find anything of interest, despite her eagle-eyed searching.

James had to smile at the disappointment on Henri's face. He was sure she had been hoping to stumble across something left behind by those who had used the watchtower before its collapse: a weapon of some kind, a piece of armour, an antique coin, or even just something from everyday life.

He had suffered the same disappointment the first time he explored the ruin, hoping to discover some trinket he could take home. He had even gone so far as to shift some of the fallen masonry, what he could, in the hope of finding something underneath it. All his efforts had been in vain, however.

"I know," he said. "I keep hoping I'm going to find something but..." He shrugged. "It was cleaned out years ago, probably by other kids with the same idea as you and me. If there's anything to be found, it's buried under all that." He gestured to the piles of broken masonry. "And without a crane, it's not going to be found."

"What about the other towers? Father Jacobs said there's twelve of them, are they all empty?" Henri fervently hoped that wasn't the case. Exploring the tower had been fun, but half the fun of exploration was the possibility of discovery. It didn't matter what the discovery might be, only that one was going to be made, and since this tower had failed her in that respect, she wanted to check out at least a few of the others.

If all the towers were devoid of the rewards of exploration, though, there was little point in checking them out.

James could only shrug again. "I haven't been to all of them, only four, the ones closest to town. I didn't find anything in any of them, so I didn't bother going to the others. They're too far for me to get to easily, especially when I wasn't sure I was going to find anything."

Dispirited, Henri picked her way carefully back to the steps so she could descend to the ground, to the visible relief of Edward. When she reached him, she sat down on a convenient piece of masonry and looked around unhappily while she waited for James to join them.

"What are we going to do for the rest of the afternoon?" she asked, abandoning her seat after less than a minute. She had never been good at sitting still, and just then was no exception as she began wandering around and over the remains of the tower that lay atop the cliff.

Reluctantly, Edward admitted that he could think of nothing to do. He looked around for inspiration and found nothing. Their position on the clifftop afforded them good visibility, once they moved away from the obscuring bulk of the collapsed tower, but that didn't help since there was little to see other than the cliff, and Blighton at its foot, mostly open countryside, and the sea.

They couldn't explore the sea, for obvious reasons, Blighton was boring, and apart from a lone goat that appeared briefly from a copse of trees half a mile or so distant, there was nothing nearby that looked worth checking out.

It was up to him, James realised, to think of something for them to do, since he was more knowledgeable about the island's entertainment opportunities. The only things that came to mind, though, either wouldn't keep them occupied for long, or would take too long to get to, and would leave them with no time to enjoy themselves.

In the end, he was forced to suggest that they go back to his house for something to drink, followed by a general wandering exploration of the island around Blighton. It was the best he could come up with just then.

"We could take the ferry to Handley tomorrow if Elizabeth's knee's better. There's more to do there. There's bowling, the cinema, shops to look at."

"Okay." Edward and Henri both agreed, happy to have something to do the following day, even if it did mean getting the ferry over to the mainland.

Edward was sure Elizabeth would want to go with them even if her knee wasn't fully better if only to avoid the boredom of another day at the farm with nothing to do.

     With those decisions made, the trio left the tower and made for the cliff path so they could descend to Blighton.

11

The planned trip to the mainland the next morning didn't happen for a couple of reasons.

Elizabeth was still limping, her knee swollen uncomfortably, despite her day of rest and the first aid provided by Brenda. She couldn't walk more than a few feet without feeling a significant amount of pain.

Even if she had been able to walk okay, they wouldn't have made it across to Handley for the clouds overhead had taken the cousins' waking as a signal to burst open. The torrent slacked within minutes of beginning but didn't stop. Instead, it settled into a steady downpour that quickly soaked everything and anyone not under cover and threatened to persist all day.

None of them wanted to be out in such weather, but neither did they want to stick around the farm. If they remained there, they were likely to end up bored or being roped into helping with the chores that Brenda and Lloyd couldn't ignore just because of the weather.

After a brief discussion, followed by a phone call to James, the decision was made to spend the day at James', and Brenda was prevailed upon to take them down there. It was an errand she agreed to without complaint, though Lloyd did comment that she was not a taxi service, and there were more important things for her to do around the farm.

Once at James' they spent the day watching DVDs, playing games on his PlayStation 2 — when they saw how embarrassed James was about the age of his console, they made sure not to make any comments that might upset him — and doing whatever else they could to entertain themselves.

Fortunately, despite the age of the console and the limited selection of games and DVDs in the Allen house, they were able to keep themselves occupied.

A LITTLE BEFORE EIGHT the next morning, with the sky overhead a cloudless blue, and showing no sign of the previous day's rain, Edward, Elizabeth, Henri, and James stepped off the ferry in Handley. The return ferry was not due to leave until six in the evening, which left them with ten hours to fill with fun, and they planned to squeeze in as much as they could.

Before they got to the fun, though, Edward and Elizabeth dragged the other two into the first supermarket they came to.

Elizabeth made straight for the magazine racks. She had plenty of reading material on her tablet, but she wanted something lighter, and some puzzle books to help keep her occupied in the evenings.

Edward had more practical things in mind. He took a trolley and swiftly made his way up and down the aisles, his eyes darting this way and that in search of what he was after.

Four powerful torches, a supply of batteries, a coiled length of rope, a couple of hammers, bottles of water, and thick gloves all made their way into the trolley, along with a variety of other items.

The range and number of things he picked up amazed the others, especially since they didn't understand what it was all about.

It wasn't until they were two-thirds of the way around the shop that they got Edward to answer their questions.

"If we're going to do more exploring," he said as he pushed the trolley towards the shelves holding the first-aid items, "I think it best that we're properly equipped for it, for any eventuality that comes up. We've got torches, so we can see okay if we go down any more tunnels. Rope and hammers in case we get into any trouble, and gloves so we don't do any more damage to our hands. Plus, first-aid stuff, so if we do get any more injuries, we can do something about them."

A quick look at Elizabeth's knee, which was still badly bruised, though she could walk mostly okay now, was enough to indicate that Edward's purchases were sensible.

"Are you sure you can afford all of this?" James asked as he watched Edward unload the trolley. The total on the till quickly climbed to a figure that would have had any adult he knew concerned about their bank balance. He couldn't imagine someone only a year or so older than him being able to afford it all, especially without checking they had enough.

Edward nodded, unconcerned by the cost of his selections, and took out his debit card, one of the few useful things his parents had given him, so he could hand it to the cashier. He was just entering his PIN into the keypad when Henri pushed through the small group and hurried away back through the shop.

"Where are you going?" Edward called after her, but she either didn't hear him or she chose not to respond for she disappeared down an aisle without responding.

"Where do you think she's gone?" Elizabeth asked once Edward had finished at the till and the two of them, with James, had moved out of the way so the next customer could be served.

"No idea," Edward said, "but knowing her, she's probably gone to get some chocolate or something." He wasn't entirely convinced by his own explanation for there was a display stand between the till he had used and the one next to it that had plenty of chocolate.

"Maybe." Elizabeth looked as unsure as her brother. "Whatever she's gone for, I wish she'd told us instead of running off like that. I don't want to spend all day here."

It was almost five minutes before Henri reappeared, a carrier bag swinging lazily from one hand and endangering the shoppers she dodged in and out of on her way to where her cousins and James were standing.

"Looks like you're right," James said when Henri got closer. He could just make out the colours of a packet of chocolate through the thin plastic of the carrier bag. "I think she's got some Minstrels and some Revels."

The moment Henri re-joined them Edward exercised his curiosity, "What did you go running off to get chocolate for? There was chocolate right by the till."

Henri grinned. "I didn't go running off for chocolate. I went to get something you didn't think of. I just saw the chocolate on my way back and decided to get some. I got Revels, Minstrels, and Malteasers, and a strawberry milkshake."

Edward couldn't imagine what he might have forgotten that Henri had thought of. Nothing important, he was sure, but he had to ask.

"This." In answer to the question, Henri reached into her carrier and pulled out a cellophane-wrapped box, which she held out to Edward. "You didn't think to get a dongle so we can get an internet signal out at the farm." She was proud of herself for having thought of it, especially when it clearly hadn't occurred to either Edward or Elizabeth, both of whom were supposed to be cleverer than her. "All we've got to do is plug it into a laptop, and then we can connect our tablets to the wireless network it creates.

"The signal might not be great, but at least we'll have one, and we won't have to be without the internet for the next six weeks."

There was silence for a few moments as Edward read the details on the box, confirming that what Henri had said was true. It wasn't that he distrusted or disbelieved her, he just wanted to be sure her excitement hadn't run away with her.

Once he was satisfied Henri was right and they would be able to get an internet signal using the dongle, without the hassle of signing up to a long-term contract, not that that would have been a real problem, more of a minor inconvenience, he returned the box.

"Nice one," he said with a smile and a nod of his head. "It didn't even occur to me to look for one of those things," he admitted, reflecting that that was probably because he was too used to being in places where there was always an internet connection available. All he had ever needed to do was either select an open connection or pay for short-term access to a closed connection.

"Nice one?" Elizabeth's tone suggested he had just offered up a vile insult rather than a compliment. "It's much better than just a nice one, it's brilliant." She threw her arms around Henri and gave her a big hug. "Thank you. I had no idea how I was going to survive out at the farm without the internet. You're amazing." After a final squeeze, she stepped back from her enormously embarrassed cousin.

"It was nothing," Henri mumbled, taken aback by the excessive display. Moving to the front of the group she led the way out of the shop, the carrier still swinging dangerously from one hand. Every so often she lifted the bottle of milkshake she held in her other hand to her lips so she could sip the pink liquid.

James acted as their guide once they were out of the shop. He didn't know the town intimately, he rarely got a chance to go there except for school, but he knew it well enough, and certainly better than the cousins.

He led them first to the bowling alley, which they had already decided they were going to do. Bowling was something they could all enjoy, even Elizabeth. The bowling alley also served food, which meant they wouldn't have to find somewhere to eat come lunchtime.

Edward won the three games they played, doing so without much difficulty for he was by far the better bowler, and once they were finished, they had lunch.

Having checked the newspaper the previous day, they knew there was an hour till the next showing of the film they had all agreed on. It wasn't enough time for them to do much, so they occupied themselves by window-shopping their way around town, which Elizabeth enjoyed more than the others, until it was time for them to go to the cinema.

James could afford his ticket, but not popcorn and a drink, and he was embarrassed when Henri, who realised why he hadn't followed her, Edward, and Elizabeth to the food counter, bought him some. He wanted to refuse, it hurt his pride to have a friend, especially a new one, buy him snacks, but she insisted, and he finally gave in.

He liked his new friends, but it was obvious they had money and were used to spending it without thought, while he had to think carefully before parting with every penny.

The previews were just starting when they found seats and they were soon engrossed in the coming attractions. In quiet tones, they discussed which of the films being previewed they might want to see and whether they would have a chance to see them before the end of the summer.

When the previews ended and the film started, they fell silent. The only noises to be heard from them those of eating and drinking, with the occasional burst of laughter or gasp of surprise as they reacted to what was happening on screen.

BRENDA WAS WAITING for them when the ferry docked. She looked curiously at the bags they were carrying but contained her curiosity, even when Edward passed his to James.

"Did you have a good time?" she asked once her charges had said goodbye to James and they were all in the Land Rover. For an answer, she received a chorus of nods and yeses. "What did you get up to?"

"We went bowling and to the cinema."

"We wandered around the shops as well," Elizabeth said, adding to her brother's brief description of their day.

"Oh, did you buy anything nice?" Brenda asked, glad of an opportunity to satisfy her curiosity about the bags the cousins had returned with.

"A few things. I bought some decent hiking boots and some clothes that will keep me from getting hurt if we go exploring again." Elizabeth wasn't thrilled by the thought of exploring but was determined to be properly equipped if they went. "I got some magazines as well, and some puzzle books."

"And I got us an internet connection," Henri said, shaking the carrier in her lap. "So we won't be bored in the evenings, or if the weather turns rubbish again."

"What about you, Edward?" Brenda asked. "Did you buy anything?"

"I bought a couple of things for when we go exploring again, mostly just some first-aid things and bottles of water," Edward said. "James said he'd look after it for us since he's our guide. Oh, I got some magazines as well."

"I hope you didn't spend all the money you've got for the holidays," Brenda said, trying not to sound overly concerned. Their parents had given her and Lloyd a more than generous sum to pay for the cousins' lodging with them, far more than it was going to cost to feed and look after them, but they had been assured that the trio had enough money to buy whatever they wanted and wouldn't need pocket money.

Brenda sincerely, though without malice, hoped that was the case. She and Lloyd would help them out if they ran short of money, and would do so willingly, nonetheless, they had plans for the money left over when the teens went home, and the more that was left the better.

Edward shook his head. "No chance of that," he said with a slightly bitter smile that surprised Brenda. "Mum and dad like to make up for not being around much by giving us lots of pocket money, and we never spend anywhere close to all of it."

In the back, Elizabeth looked sadly out the window next to her, while Henri bobbed her head up and down in agreement with Edward. Brenda saw both reactions in the rear-view mirror and couldn't help feeling bad for the cousins. Money was not, and never could be, adequate compensation for a parent's absence.

"My parents are the worst," Henri said. "Well, unless you count Obnoxious Ollie's. His parents get him whatever he wants, no matter how stupid it is." She remembered her cousin asking for a Vietnamese pot-bellied pig once, just because he had seen a celebrity on TV with one. The next week he had one and it had proceeded to cause more than ten thousand pounds worth of damage to the house and landscaped gardens. "Mine give me fifty pounds a week pocket money, and another fifty pounds for every week they don't get a phone call about me from school. And two hundred and fifty pounds for every 'A' I get in a class."

"I don't suppose they have to pay that bonus very often," Elizabeth couldn't help saying.

Henri grinned as she shook her head. "Not often, no. Cs and Bs are my level. Occasionally I get lucky and get an A, but it's usually only in history, and once in a blue moon in maths. It's just as well your parents don't do the same thing; it'd cost them a fortune for a smarty-pants like you."

There was no malice in the comment, as Elizabeth well knew, so she didn't take offence.

"Did you have anything to eat this afternoon?" Brenda asked, changing the subject to something she found less disturbing.

"We had lunch at the bowling alley, and popcorn at the cinema," Henri said.

Brenda smiled. "I guess you won't want any dinner then."

"I'm not hungry," Elizabeth said, but she was the only one.

Edward and Henri both declared that they still had space for dinner, though not a big one.

12

The rest of the week passed in a similar vein to the beginning, with their days split between exploring various parts of the island, the parts they could get to without transport, playing on James' PlayStation 2, and another trip to the mainland for the cinema.

The days passed quickly, with every moment that could be, filled with whatever entertainment they could find or imagine.

The result was that although they acquired a few more scrapes and bruises and were exhausted by the time they went to bed each night, they enjoyed themselves. None of them, least of all Elizabeth, admitted as much, but they had more fun when they went exploring than when they played on James' console or went to the cinema.

The watchtowers continued to be disappointingly free of relics for them to find, having been picked clean by successive generations of kids with the same idea. They harboured vague hopes of finding something in at least one of the remaining watchtowers, most likely in the one farthest from Blighton, the distance to which they thought might have kept all but the most enthusiastic of relic hunters from exploring it. How they were going to get to that watchtower, though, they hadn't figured out.

The island itself more than made up for the lack of relics or treasure. Even when they came across one of the houses abandoned by the diminishing population, they found beauty and things to like: flowers, wildlife, and nature in its various forms.

SATURDAY FOUND EDWARD, Elizabeth, Henri, and James doing

something different.

The four of them sat around one of the small tables in the library, each occupied in different ways.

James was using the library's computer to surf the internet and mess about on social media, which the frustratingly slow internet at home made difficult. Not that the internet in the library was much quicker.

Edward was trying to identify the various birds and animals they had come across during the week. He had taken pictures of them all and was now leafing through books to discover what they were, and if there was anything special about them.

Elizabeth was at James' side, using her tablet to surf the internet on the library's Wi-Fi, though they had wildly different ideas about what to surf for. She didn't need to catch up with her social media because the dongle Henri had bought enabled her to do so at the farm, so she was watching videos on YouTube and looking for anything else that might interest her.

Henri in the meantime was, unusually, being studious. She was reading up on the history of Bligh Island and the Bligh family.

The four of them had been in the library for over an hour, without having seen anyone, even Mrs Neill, the librarian, for most of that time when Father Jacobs strode in. He looked flushed and had to take a few moments to regain his breath, as though he had been hurrying.

"There you are," he said finally.

"Were you looking for us?" Edward asked, glancing up from the book he was using to try to identify a small snake he had photographed the day before. He wondered why the priest would have been hurrying to find them and couldn't think of a reason.

"Yes," Father Jacobs said with a nod. "I called your aunt and she told me where to find you all."

"Why were you looking for us?"

All four teens looked curiously at the priest. Despite his haste to find them, he gave no sign of being the bearer of bad news. The truth was quite the opposite in fact.

"How would you like to visit the family home?" Father Jacobs asked. When he realised that he hadn't been understood, he clarified, "I've managed to get permission for you all to look around the castle before it opens for tourist season on Monday. Are you interested?" There was no need for the teens to answer him, the looks on their faces did that.

THE DRIVE TO BLIGH Castle, as it was called, took a little over half an hour in Father Jacobs' battered old Citroen, which protested every inch of the climb to the top of the cliff, though it drove fine after that.

Elizabeth, Henri, and James, who had been squashed together in the back of the car, all gave exaggerated sighs of relief once they were able to get out.

After stretching to ease their cramped muscles, they followed Father Jacobs across the car park to the huge double doors, which were made of oak and bound in iron, just like those of the church, though about twice the size.

Only a battering ram, or a cannon, was likely to get the doors open when they were barred, which the teens were sure was the intention, and there was no knocker with which to get anyone's attention.

Father Jacobs showed no concern over the large barrier that stood between the group and the castle grounds. He didn't even allow the sight of it to slow him.

There was a small door set within the larger doors, and he reached out a hand to it as he got closer. It swung open easily at his touch.

The cousins and James followed Father Jacobs through the door and found themselves in a spacious courtyard, surrounded on three sides by the high and solidly built walls that had protected the castle since it was built. On the fourth side of the courtyard was Bligh Castle.

The castle was imposing, and it was clear that the building and its surrounding wall had been constructed with defence in mind. In that respect, the builders had more than achieved their goal.

The castle, its battlements, and the walls were solidly constructed, and gave off an air of impenetrability and permanence, as if neither time, weather, nor the destructiveness of man could have any effect on them.

If there was one thing the castle was missing, it was a sense of welcome.

Father Jacobs had said that the castle had been occupied by the Bligh family for four and a half centuries, without a break, right up until the nineteen-forties, and that it was now administered by the National Trust as a tourist attraction. Despite that, it seemed more like it anticipated the arrival of an attacking army than welcome guests.

Once through the doors to the castle itself, which stood open, it all changed.

The interior showed the centuries of making the place a home. Carpets and rugs covered the floors, paintings hung on the walls, depicting the various barons and their families and scenes from history, and other signs of being lived in were to be seen around the place, relieving the bare stone.

The group was greeted, briefly, by the leader of the National Trust team who administered the castle, but were then left to wander wherever they wished, so long as they were careful.

"It's because you're direct descendants of the baron," Father Jacobs explained when Elizabeth expressed her surprise at the freedom they were being given. "According to the agreement that loans the castle to the National Trust, any direct descendant may visit the castle any time they wish and go wherever they want. And since I've agreed to show you around, and the trust team knows me, there's no need for any of them to escort you to make sure you don't take or damage anything." He fixed James with a stern look as he said that, though it was clear that he wasn't being serious.

The obvious starting place for their tour was the great hall, so named because it was the largest room in the castle and the place where the baron had held both banquets and court.

As Father Jacobs explained while leading the quartet of teens from one room to the next, the layout of the castle was similar to that of many other castles to be found around the United Kingdom.

"Baron Edward was interested in defence, rather than originality," he said. "And instructed his architect to go with a tried and tested design. It was the right choice. The castle walls have never been breached. Though to be fair, no one ever made a serious effort to do so." He would have liked it if there had been a battle for the castle at some point in the past, it would have made the history of the island that much more exciting.

Every room they were taken to held something of interest for at least one of them.

Elizabeth enjoyed the paintings, decorations, and costumes, while Edward was fascinated by the history of the family and the castle, as revealed by almost everything, but especially by the display cabinets, where special items could be seen, with cards revealing their name, age, origin, and use.

Henri and James were also interested in the historical aspects of what Father Jacobs showed them, history was after all Henri's best subject at school, but it was the weapons that they liked the most.

On the walls, and in a variety of cases, were displayed swords, knives, maces, muskets, and virtually every other type of weapon that might have been used from the fourteen-hundreds onwards.

The highlights of the day, at least as far as Henri and James were concerned, were being allowed out onto the battlements atop the castle and down into the armoury.

Elizabeth found the armoury boring since weapons didn't interest her and there was a strong smell of must and rust, but she enjoyed the view from the battlements.

While in the armoury, Henri couldn't resist taking down one of the swords from a rack. It was lighter than she expected, and she almost knocked over the rack it had come from when it swung easily in her grasp. She doubted she could have wielded it in combat for long for light as it was, it was still heavy enough to wear her down quickly, but she was pleased to be able to wield it at all.

"It was designed to be used by a man," Father Jacobs pointed out once all the teens had taken their turn with the sword and it had been returned to the rack. "Any man training to be a warrior would have begun that training at the age of about five or six. They would have spent several hours every day working with swords of gradually increasing weight, starting with wooden swords, to strengthen the young warrior's muscles until he could wield a full-sized and properly weighted weapon.

"By the time he was your age, Edward, he would be expected to fight with a sword like that one." He indicated the weapon tested by them all. "How skilful he might be with the sword would, of course, depend on how naturally adept he was, and how much attention he paid to his training. He would be expected to at least be able to wield the sword and defend himself with it. He might even have to do so in combat if the castle was attacked, or he was needed to bolster the numbers in a battle.

"I guess you could consider the training similar to what a professional footballer or athlete goes through. If they want to be good, they have to start young."

"What about girls?" Henri asked. "When would they have started their training?"

"Don't be daft," Elizabeth told her. "Girls didn't get to use swords. I thought you knew history. Boys got to be warriors, and girls had to look after the children and do all the cooking and cleaning."

Father Jacobs nodded. "That's mostly true, though it did depend on the status of the girl or woman. A high-born girl or woman would be expected to marry well for the benefit of her family, and to spend her days weaving, embroidering, or keeping herself occupied with whatever activity was fashionable at the time. She would also have to learn the art of managing a household, though if she were sufficiently high-born and rich there would be a servant to handle the day-to-day running of things."

Henri looked disgruntled at the thought of what she would have been expected to do had she been born in another era. Marriage was one thing, she hadn't made up her mind on that, but being expected to spend her time doing embroidery or something similar was too dreadful for her to contemplate.

"WELL, WHAT DO YOU THINK of the family home?" Father Jacobs asked as they drove away from the castle, almost three hours after arriving.

Elizabeth was disappointed and didn't hesitate to say so. "I know it's a castle, not a stately home, but I thought it was going to be more like Downton Abbey. I wouldn't want to live there, it'd be creepy, especially at night. I did like the old costumes. It would be fun to be able to try them on whenever I want and pretend I'm back in the olden days with knights and ladies. And the beds..." She sighed at the memory of the four-poster beds that had been in many of the bedrooms used by the family.

"What about the rest of you?"

"I've seen it before," James said, having come out to the castle with his aunt when he was younger. "It was great to see the bits that are normally off-limits, though. I didn't expect there to be so many weapons in the armoury, you could have equipped a small army."

"That was the idea," Father Jacobs said. "The castle used to house an army, so they needed to be able to arm them. It wasn't as large an army as you might expect to see today, but it was several hundred strong, and they had to have enough weapons for all of them, plus spares.

"Even in the First World War, they had fifty soldiers stationed at the castle, along with a Royal Navy ship in the bay, to prevent the island and the castle falling into enemy hands."

"Why would they have bothered?" Edward asked. "There's nothing worth worrying about here."

"Nothing but its location," Father Jacobs said. "But sometimes that's enough. The island may not be much, but it does command a good position. If the Germans had taken the island, they could have used artillery to cause problems for both the Royal Navy and civilian shipping, potentially starving the UK into submission. They could even have used the island as a staging post for an invasion of Southern England." He turned his attention to the youngest of his passengers then. "What did you think of the castle?"

"It was very cool," Henri said enthusiastically. "I wish the family still lived there. I'd never get bored with so much great stuff to play with, and so many places to explore. It'd take ages to explore the whole castle and discover everything."

13

"Why do you want me to let you out here?" Father Jacobs asked as he pulled his car over to the side of the road where James indicated.

He looked suspiciously at the teen in the rear of the car. He didn't doubt for a moment that the young troublemaker had something in mind, and he could only worry that James was planning something that his father, and others, wouldn't approve of if they found out about it. "There's nothing out here."

"Sure there is," James said as he got out of the car. "Solomon Kierney's place is less than a mile that way." He pointed away from the road, though he was aware that nothing was visible in that direction. "I thought they'd like to see it since we're so close. We can walk to their aunt and uncle's from there, it's not far."

Father Jacobs looked around at the cousins. "Do you want to get out here and go with James to see what's left of Solomon Kierney's house, or would you rather I drive you back to the farm?" He could understand the appeal of the house that had been used by Kierney and his gang of smugglers, from a historian's point of view, but he couldn't imagine it being of much interest to anyone else since it was a ruin.

Henri nodded without hesitation and quickly got out of the car to join James at the side of the road.

Edward, after a moment's thought, decided that he too would like to see the house.

Elizabeth, however, preferred to go back to the farm. She had had enough of exercise and exploring for one day and wanted nothing more than to relax with a book.

Edward, James, and Henri watched for a few moments as Father

Jacobs drove off down the road, taking Elizabeth back to the Bligh farm, and then James turned away to lead the other two across country towards their unseen destination.

The land was largely flat, leaving the cousins to wonder how there could be a building out there, even if it was nearly a mile away, without them being able to see it. The only thing they could see was a copse of trees in the distance, but they didn't imagine it was hiding the smuggler's house since they weren't heading in that direction.

They trusted James enough to follow him, however, their pace slow as they watched for anything that might trip them up.

"WHAT HAPPENED TO IT?" Henri asked when they reached the ruins of what might, once, have been a nice house.

"Apparently, Kierney rigged a boobytrap whenever he left the house on a smuggling run. After he was caught, the customs people tried to break into the house to find his tunnel. They triggered the boobytrap and it started a fire that burned the house down," James said.

Henri grinned, amused by the thought of the smuggler getting one over on the customs people one last time.

"After the fire went out the house was searched. Father J says the customs people wanted to block the tunnel to stop anyone else using it for smuggling."

"Didn't you say the other day that the entrance to the tunnels was never found?" Edward asked.

James nodded. "Yeah. The customs people searched the ruins. Father J's searched them, and so have others over the years. No one's ever found the entrance, though. They haven't found the entrance at the bottom of the cliff either. Most people think the booby trap destroyed the entrances, either because Kierney didn't want the customs people to use them as proof he was a smuggler, or because he had the bulk of his money hidden in the tunnels and he wanted to be able to recover it later."

"Maybe it did," Edward said, thinking that if Kierney had been clever enough to rig a boobytrap that could burn his house down to try and conceal his smuggling, he was almost certainly clever enough to make sure the entrances to the tunnels were destroyed as well. "Or maybe there never was a way into the tunnels from the house. Maybe everyone's been looking in the wrong place."

"P'raps. But I think it's here, somewhere, under all that, and one day I'm going to find it," James said determinedly, as though he was intending to find a treasure that would make him rich. "Just like I'm going to find the path down to the cave." He saw the confused looks that came his way from Edward and Henri and went on. "The cave the smugglers used is supposed to be at the base of the cliff, over this way, and there's a path leading down to it. At least according to what I've heard. Even if you can find the path, though, you're only supposed to be able to get to the cave at low tide, unless you're in a boat and you know the way through the rocks out there."

By then James had led them over to the edge of the cliff and, looking down, they could see the white spray that shot into the air whenever a wave broke against one of the rocks that lay just beneath the surface of the water. Most of the rocks were out of sight, but they didn't need to be able to see them to know that the area was littered with hazards, the volume of white spray that hung in the air revealed their presence.

"How come you haven't found the path if it's here?" Henri asked.

James shrugged. "It's here," he said with certainty. "I know it is. Part of the cliff edge collapsed at some point, and I think it took the start of the path with it. I have a look for it every time I come out this way in case I get lucky." So saying, he strolled off along the cliff edge, his eyes on the ground as he searched for the elusive path that would lead him to the cave he was so desperate to find.

Edward wanted to order Henri away from the edge before she
fell or the ground collapsed beneath her, but he sensibly chose not to
waste his breath. It was an order he knew would not be obeyed, no
matter how well-intentioned the thought behind it, so he settled for
cautioning her to be careful and to watch her feet.

He watched for several long moments to be sure Henri had listened
to him, and then he turned away from the cliff edge so he could return
to the burnt-out house. He didn't imagine he was going to find the
tunnel entrance James had mentioned, he couldn't even make up his
mind whether he believed it existed, but he felt an urge to poke around
the charred remains anyway.

His hands and jeans were both black from dirt and soot, though he
had nothing to show for the state he had got himself in, when a shout
from the cliff edge sent him running from the ruined house.

His heart was in his mouth as he saw that what he had feared had
come to pass. Henri had either slipped, or the ground had collapsed
under her. All he could see of her was her arm, and all that was keeping
her from being crushed against the base of the cliff by the rolling waves
was James' hold on her wrist as he desperately struggled to pull her back
up.

Despite running as fast as he could, Edward was still ten yards away
when James lost his grip and Henri's hand slid through his.

With a scream that was cut off abruptly, Henri fell.

Edward felt his heart plummet with his cousin. He had been aware
of the risk, had even warned her about it, but he still couldn't believe
Henri had fallen.

"Henri!" he yelled, panic-stricken. Falling to his knees at the cliff
edge, he crawled forward slowly and carefully so he could peer down
in the desperate hope of a miracle. "Henri!" he called again, wondering
how he was going to explain what had happened to Brenda and Lloyd,
let alone to Elizabeth, his parents, and to Henri's parents.

"Ed!"

Edward was both shocked and relieved to hear his cousin's voice, which startled him so much that for a moment he thought he was going to lose his balance and follow her over the edge. He hastily backed up until he felt safer, and then slowly eased forward again so he could take another look over the edge.

"Henri, are you down there?" he called out, leaning forward a little farther.

The reply came after several long seconds.

"Yes, I'm here," Henri said in a voice that shook from a mixture of fear and relief.

"Are you alright?" Edward felt stupid the moment the question left his lips. "Are you hurt?"

"No, not really," Henri called back. "Just shaken up, and I twisted my ankle."

Edward felt a fresh wave of relief wash over him. "Where are you?" He still couldn't see any sign of her, despite him leaning so far out that James had to grab him by the back of his t-shirt to keep him from falling.

"Here." A dirty hand waved from a spot about ten feet below and half a dozen feet to one side.

"How did you end up there? No, scratch that, it doesn't matter. Stay there, I'll get help." Explanations, Edward realised, could wait until Henri was safe.

After backing far enough away from the edge to feel safe doing so, Edward got to his feet. He took out his mobile phone while looking around futilely for someone, preferably an adult, who could help rescue Henri, all the time berating himself for having left the supplies he had bought in Handley at James'. Neither the rope nor the other items he had bought to help them with their exploring were of any use if they didn't have them to hand.

There was no one to be seen, unfortunately, only a pair of horses, and since they didn't have ropes or anything else that might be useful in a rescue, they were of no help.

Under normal circumstances, Edward felt more grown-up, if not fully adult, than most kids his age, and he would have been prepared to tell anyone who asked that he could handle pretty much any situation he might encounter. Just then, though, he was willing to admit that he was not as capable as he had believed.

Time and again he tried to call the farm, without success. He didn't have so much as a single bar of signal, making it impossible for him to get a connection, let alone get hold of anyone.

After multiple failed attempts to make a phone call, Edward turned to James. "You said it's only about a mile from here to the farm?" He was so concerned for Henri that he was surprised he had remembered what James had said.

James nodded, his head bobbing up and down rapidly like it was on a spring. "Yeah, about a mile that way." He pointed inland and to the North without hesitation.

"Good, go there as quickly as you can, tell Brenda and Lloyd what's happened and get help," Edward said hurriedly. That done, he turned back to the cliff edge so he could let Henri know what was going on. "James is going to the farm to get help. He'll be back soon." He hoped the news would reassure her that she would soon be rescued.

"It's alright," Henri called back, sounding calmer than she had before. "I think I've found the path James was looking for. I might be able to get out of here myself."

"What do you mean?" Edward got back on his knees and then down onto his belly, so he could wriggle forward as far as he felt it was safe to do, and then a little further.

He didn't feel all that safe, especially when the blood rushed to his head as he leant out over the edge, trying to glimpse Henri. He decided the risk and the dizziness were worth it, though, when he caught sight of the blue t-shirt Henri was wearing. He couldn't see her fully, but he could see her well enough to tell that she was moving slowly to his left.

"What are you doing?" He tried to keep the panic he felt at the thought of Henri putting herself in more danger by moving around at a minimum, to avoid alarming her.

James had started for the farm but when he heard about the path he turned around and came back.

Henri's voice drifted up again. "The path goes up and down by the look of it. I'm going to see where it leads." The sound of tumbling stones, followed a short while later by a distant splash, came from the general direction of her position. "See if there's a way up to the top of the cliff."

Edward wanted to tell her to stay where she was, to keep still and not take any kind of risk in case she made her situation worse. He didn't, though. As much as he wanted to, he realised that if there was a way to the top, or even just a way to get closer to it, it would be easier to rescue her.

"Be careful," he called to her. "If you feel the ground moving, stop straight away."

The ten minutes that followed were the longest Edward could remember. They seemed to stretch into eternity as he strained his senses, his hearing most of all, in an effort to follow Henri's progress.

His heart beat a rapid tempo against his ribcage the whole time, increasing in speed until it threatened to beat right out of his chest whenever he heard the slither of stones or a cry of alarm.

His concerns didn't diminish when Henri shouted up to tell him that her route disappeared into the cliff and away from the fresh air. He no longer had to worry that she was going to fall into the surf and be crushed against the cliff, but he did have to worry that the cliff might collapse on her or she might get stuck.

"Do you think she's alright?" James asked nervously when a couple of minutes passed without them hearing anything from Henri, good or bad, despite their shouts.

Edward shrugged uncertainly. He hadn't heard or felt anything to suggest that the tunnel had collapsed on Henri, or that anything else bad had happened to her, but the lack of a response to his shouts worried him greatly, and it must have shown on his face.

"I'll get Brenda and Lloyd," James said, turning from the cliff edge so he could run for the farm.

He ran as fast as he could, heedless of the possibility that he might catch his foot on something and go flying, hoping as he ran that he hadn't left it too late to get help for his friend by waiting to see if she could find her way to the top of the cliff.

"Henri!" Edward yelled, desperate to hear a response, any kind of response, so long as it told him she was still alive. "Henri! Can you hear me?" He lifted his voice until he was sure he could have been heard by everyone on the island.

Faintly, so faintly that he would have missed it if there had been a single other sound stirring on the air, Edward heard his cousin's voice.

"Ed."

It came not from the direction of the cliff edge, as he expected it to, but from a short distance inland.

"Henri!" he called again at the top of his lungs before cocking his head to listen intently.

"Ed." The call was louder and more distinct this time.

"Henri," Edward called once more, walking slowly in the direction Henri's voice had come from. He followed her voice, which grew steadily louder and nearer, until he saw a small gorse bush move in a way that couldn't be explained by the breeze.

The bush moved again, as though someone was trying to uproot it from below, and then Henri's head popped up through the branches like a jack-in-the-box.

The suddenness of her appearance startled Edward and he jumped in surprise.

Once he recovered, he felt a wave of relief sweep through him. It subsided after a moment and he hurried forward to help Henri climb out from beneath the bush, which wasn't easy for the hole the bush concealed had partially collapsed at some point, making it barely wide enough for her.

"Are you alright?" Edward pulled his cousin up and into a hug. He released her almost immediately so he could look her up and down, checking for any visible injuries.

Henri nodded. "I'm fine." She corrected herself almost immediately. "A little shaken up actually, and my ankle hurts," she admitted, "but given I fell off a cliff." She gave a quick laugh that wobbled a little. "I could, and probably should, be a whole lot worse off." Absently she brushed herself off, removing what of the dirt that stained her clothes she could.

14

"You could have been badly hurt. You could have been killed."

Henri sighed heavily as she looked up from her tablet. She couldn't believe Elizabeth still hadn't let the subject drop.

It was the repetition, rather than her cousin's insistence on talking about what had happened, that annoyed her the most. It wouldn't have been half so bad if Elizabeth could just think of something different to say, she thought. She couldn't, though. She had been saying the same thing again and again, with almost no variation, since they came upstairs and got into bed.

Worse than that, everything Elizabeth was saying then she had already said upon reaching the spot where Henri had nearly lost her life that afternoon.

JAMES HAD MADE IT TO the farm in record time. Unfortunately, neither Brenda nor Lloyd had been at the house, only Elizabeth, and she hadn't known where on the farm they were.

Elizabeth had wanted to call Constable Lewis or Father Jacobs, or any other adult who might be able to help. James, however, had thought it better simply to grab some rope and hurry back to do what they could.

In his opinion, Constable Lewis was next to useless and would be no help, assuming they were able to convince him they were telling the truth, and Father Jacobs or anyone else they called would want to waste time calling Constable Lewis.

Any delay, and there had been enough of one already, could prove fatal.

That argument had persuaded Elizabeth and together they had hurried to the clifftop near Solomon Kierney's house, only to find that the emergency was over, and Henri was safe.

Elizabeth's relief had lasted for only a few moments and then she began berating her brother, her cousin, and James for allowing the situation to occur.

James had moved away almost immediately to examine the hole through which Henri had reappeared. He wasn't interested in being told off by a girl who was only a year older than him.

The moment he saw the hole, and the bush that concealed it, he realised why he had failed to find the start of the path that led down to the cave Solomon Kierney and his gang of smugglers had used. He had been looking along the edge of the cliff when the start of the path was almost thirty yards back from it. Even if he had searched inland from the cliff's edge, he doubted he would have found what he was looking for.

He wondered if Kierney had planted the gorse bush to prevent the customs people from finding it, or if it was mere coincidence. He suspected the former. Planting a gorse bush to conceal a secret seemed like the kind of thing that someone who had boobytrapped their own home would do.

"YOU'VE SAID THAT ALREADY, repeatedly," Henri said, tapping the screen of her tablet to pause the film she had been watching. "Can't you just let it drop? It was an accident, and my fault for getting too close to the edge. Besides, it's over with and I'm safe, and as a bonus, I found what we were looking for." She could have done without the heart-stopping fall over the cliff edge when she lost her footing, but she was pleased to have discovered the path James had been looking for.

"Was it really worth risking your life for?" Elizabeth wanted to know.

Henri grinned. "We won't know that until we explore the path and find out if it does lead to the smuggler's cave. Who knows what we might find there." Her eyes gleamed briefly at the thought of the relics, treasures, or even just trinkets they might find.

Elizabeth couldn't believe that Henri was thinking about risking herself again. "Are you crazy? After what happened today, you want to go back there?"

"Yes. You don't have to come with me and James when we check it out, it's not really your kind of thing, but I think Ed's going to come with us." Henri was sure Edward's main reason for going would be to keep her safe from harm, but she suspected he was also interested in discovering what, if anything, the smugglers had left behind.

Elizabeth put aside her tablet, threw back the duvet on her side of the bed, and got to her feet. In moments she was across the room and out the door.

Henri didn't need to ask or follow to know where she was going. Elizabeth was going to talk to Edward, to try to persuade him to stop her exploring the smugglers' trail. Fat chance of that, she thought.

If they believed it was too dangerous and didn't want to take the risk, that was up to them, but she wasn't going to let them decide what she could or couldn't do. They weren't her parents, even if they sometimes acted as though they were. They weren't even adults, not that she would have listened to any who did try to stop her.

15

When morning arrived, Henri discovered that Elizabeth didn't need Edward's help to block the planned exploration. Circumstances themselves were against it, at least for that day.

"Henri, it's James," Brenda called down the passage to the kitchen from the telephone, which had disturbed breakfast, to the annoyance of Lloyd, who looked on disapprovingly as Henri got to her feet so she could take the call.

"Hi," Henri said the moment she took the phone. "What's up?" She was sure something must be since they had already arranged that James would come out to the farm for nine, so they could go to the ruins of Kierney's house and the tunnel she had found.

"We can't go exploring today," James said miserably. "I've been grounded."

"What? Why?"

"Dad saw the mess my clothes were in when I got back yesterday and wasn't happy. He probably wouldn't have been so bothered if they'd just been dirty, but I got a couple of tears from the gorse bush as well. He saw them and went off on one. Apparently, I don't appreciate my clothes or how hard he has to work to afford them, so I'm grounded. Which means we can't go and explore that path you found to see if it does lead to Kierney's cave."

Henri was tempted to say that it meant he couldn't explore the path she had found, but she still could. She didn't see why her fun should be ruined just because he had got in trouble. She didn't, though, for she realised that it wouldn't be very nice of her, especially since James had had his heart set on finding the cave used by Kierney and his gang of smugglers for years.

"How long are you grounded for?"

"I don't know," James admitted. "Dad never tells me how long I'm grounded for. He says it's not a proper punishment if I know how long it's going to last for."

Henri was silent for a moment and then she said, "I guess we'll have to wait until you're no longer grounded to check the path out." She would just have to be patient, she thought.

They talked for a while longer and then she hung up so she could return to her breakfast, which she suspected had gone cold in the time she had been on the phone.

Since her original plan for the day was out the window, Henri was left with little choice about how to spend her day. She could stay at the farm, where there was a good chance she would either end up bored or roped into doing chores — it wasn't that she was averse to helping out on the farm, she thought it might even be fun if tiring, but it wasn't what she had planned for the day — or she could go with Brenda, who had announced that she needed to go to the mainland to get some things.

She might have chosen to stay at the farm to help out, especially if it meant making sure Babs hadn't escaped again or feeding the piglets, which she found cute. Edward and Elizabeth had both decided to go with Brenda, though, and Henri didn't fancy being the only one to stay behind with Lloyd, whom she found too gruff compared to Brenda.

THE NEXT MORNING, HENRI phoned James first thing, before she sat down to breakfast. She hoped to find that his father had relented, and his punishment was over. Unfortunately, she soon learned that that was not the case.

Not only was James still grounded, but he wasn't even allowed to the phone to speak to her. Henri took that as a bad sign.

With exploring the tunnel and cave still out of the question, she decided there was only one thing she and her cousins could do to occupy themselves.

The leader of the National Heritage team at the castle had said they were welcome back whenever they wanted to visit, and as members of the Bligh family they could go anywhere they wished, so long as they were careful. It was an invitation Henri decided they would take up.

It had been fun being shown around by Father Jacobs and told all the stories he knew, but she thought it would be more fun to check out the castle without supervision. She hoped to find some hidden passages or other secrets that had been forgotten about.

Edward and Elizabeth agreed to Henri's suggestion of visiting the castle readily since neither of them could think of anything else to do.

As on their previous visit, the small door in the huge double gate was unsecured and swung open at a touch, and the double doors of the castle proper stood open in welcome.

They walked straight in and then spent the better part of half an hour searching for the National Heritage team to let them know they were there, in case anything happened.

Once they found the team, who were hard at work cleaning the kitchen, as though it was to be used by a top chef, Edward, Elizabeth, and Henri set off to explore.

Edward and Elizabeth decided to tour the ground floor, starting at the main entrance, so they could explore each room in more detail than had been possible while Father Jacobs was escorting them.

Henri chose not to stick with her cousins, figuring she would either get bored or annoyed if she did. Instead, she found her way to the stairs that led down to the cellar and the armoury. She half-expected to find the door locked, given that the castle's valuable collection of wine and dangerous collection of weapons were to be found down there but it wasn't.

The stairs were dark, so she left the door at the top standing open to help her see as she descended. When she got to the bottom, she had to fumble around for a few moments before finding the switch to the electric lights that had been fitted at some point in the past.

She assumed the lights had been installed by the family before the second world war for the dustiness of the cellar, especially the armoury and its contents, suggested it wasn't included on any tour of the castle.

Once in the armoury, she made straight for the sword she had wielded during her previous visit. It surprised her again how light the sword was, compared to her expectations. She had always thought that swords were heavy things that only a grown man could lift or swing.

She could lift the sword, but after just a couple of swings, she felt her muscles straining and had to return it to the rack. It frustrated her to think that she couldn't even pretend to be a warrior, a role she much preferred over that of a useless high-born lady doing needlework, but then she remembered Arya Stark from Game of Thrones.

Henri knew she wasn't supposed to watch Game of Thrones, she was too young, but her parents had never shown any concern over what she watched, so long as she kept out of their way and didn't get in trouble.

She had quickly come to love the character of Arya Stark, who was exactly the sort of person she would have wanted to be if she lived in a fantasy world, a warrior and a fighter who didn't let anyone tell her what she could or couldn't do.

In remembering Arya Stark, Henri recalled that the sword she carried was not a longsword like she had been trying to wield, but a weapon with a narrow blade that was light enough for her to use effectively.

Turning away from the rack of longswords, she began searching the armoury for a more suitable weapon, something she could wield more easily. Given the variety of weapons in the armoury, she was sure she would find something.

She did, though it took her a while.

Almost hidden behind a full suit of armour that looked as though it weighed several times what she did was a rack that held several slender swords.

Henri didn't have a clue what the different types of sword in the rack were called, but neither did she care. All that mattered to her was that all the swords looked more suited to her size and strength.

She examined the swords on the rack and selected the one that looked most like the weapon Arya Stark carried. Taking it down she swung it experimentally and found it much easier to use than the longsword.

As she moved around the armoury, slashing and cutting at the air, Henri tried to think of a way for her to sneak the sword back to the farm, and ultimately get it home. She was confident she could learn to use the sword properly, given enough time and practice, even if the only reason for her to do so was for the pleasure of knowing how to fight with a sword.

After a couple of minutes, she realised it would require more risk and hassle than it was worth to sneak the sword home. As fun as it would be to have a sword she could wield like a warrior, it would almost certainly get her into trouble, either with her parents or with someone else.

She was used to being in trouble, but she did know where to draw the line, and being found in possession of a potentially deadly weapon was more trouble than she wanted.

"WHAT ON EARTH HAVE you been up to?" Elizabeth wanted to know when she caught sight of Henri.

Henri was sweaty and flushed, her clothes were filthy and torn, and she had cobwebs in her hair, but she was grinning broadly.

"I was having fun," she said.

"Having fun? What do you mean, 'having fun'? What kind of fun leaves you looking like that?" Elizabeth knew she shouldn't be surprised, given how her cousin was. Somehow, though, Henri's appearance still startled her, as it did Edward, who was looking at Henri in displeased amazement.

Henri glanced down at herself, as if unaware of the state she was in. Her grin broadened as she looked up again. "The best kind. I found a sword I could swing and was pretending to be Arya Stark. It was great. Then I found the dungeons." She was pleased with herself for having made that discovery.

"What dungeons?" Edward asked, unable to conceal his interest. "Father Jacobs never said anything about there being dungeons."

"Maybe he doesn't know about them," Henri said, though she thought it unlikely, given everything else the priest knew about the island, the castle, and the Bligh family. She thought it more likely that he had simply decided not to tell them about an aspect of their family's history that was probably less than pleasant. "You get to them through a door at the very back of the cellar. It's partly hidden behind some old barrels." She had only found it because she had been searching the cellar in the hope of finding a hidden door or a secret compartment or something. "There was a room for guards or something, and on the other side of it was the stairs leading down to the dungeon."

"What was it like down there?" Edward found the thought of dungeons beneath a medieval castle frightening and exciting in equal measure.

"Dark," Henri said honestly. "I couldn't really see anything. And it's smelly. Worse than the pigpen." The disgust on Elizabeth's face made her smile. Elizabeth had developed a strong dislike for the smell that came from the pigpen, and Henri suspected she would feel sick if she made it as far as the doorway leading down to the dungeon. "We'll have to come back with torches when James is no longer grounded, there's no light down there at all. I only know it's a dungeon because of what I could see in the light from my phone."

16

Edward, Elizabeth, and Henri had started along the road from the castle to Blighton at a quick pace. They were hungry and eager to get back to the farm as soon as they could.

Their hunger, like their pace, soon subsided, though, as they became immersed in the peace and quiet of their surroundings.

Aside from the castle, there was not a building in sight. Nor was there any other sign of humanity. All there was to see was nature, mostly in the form of heathland dotted with gorse bushes, but there was a copse of trees in the distance, and the occasional animal.

They mostly saw rabbits and horses, but they also caught sight of a pair of deer and some free-roaming sheep.

There was barely a breeze at ground level, but up above, dark clouds were being blown across the sky, threatening rain. It was a threat that was soon delivered on as the clouds burst open, unleashing a steady downpour that soaked them within moments.

Elizabeth got wet the quickest thanks to the light summer dress she was wearing. Despite that, she fared the best since Edward and Henri were both wearing jeans and found it hard to move as the denim got soaked and began to cling to them awkwardly.

"Is that someone over there?" Elizabeth asked, wiping the rain from her eyes so she could see better through the gloom that had descended on them, even though it was barely midday.

Edward and Henri looked where Elizabeth was pointing but couldn't make out anything.

Edward was about to remark that she must have seen an animal when a figure appeared from behind a large gorse bush.

The person, whom none of them could see clearly enough to tell whether it was male or female, was heading towards the road. When they realised that, the cousins slowed their pace.

Without knowing who the figure was or why they were out there in the middle of nowhere, they didn't want to catch up to him or her in case it was someone unfriendly.

They had enough sense not to approach a stranger without good reason at the best of times. To do so when the weather was bad and there was no one they knew around to help if they encountered trouble was crazy, especially in such an out of the way place.

It wasn't long, however, before they discovered that their caution, though sensible, was unnecessary.

"That's James," Henri said a minute or so after they first saw the figure. "James," she called out.

When James showed no sign of having heard her, Henri sucked in a lungful of air so she could call again, as loudly as she could to be heard over the rain. It wasn't necessary, however. No sooner had she opened her mouth to shout than the figure stopped at the side of the road and turned to look back through the rain.

It was then that Edward and Elizabeth saw that Henri was right, it was James.

"What are you doing here?" Henri demanded the moment they caught up with their friend. "I thought you were grounded." Her tone was suspicious and accusatory, and neither James, Edward, nor Elizabeth missed the way her eyes traced back over the route James had followed to the road, which led in the direction of Solomon Kierney's ruined house and the hidden tunnel.

"I am grounded," James said quickly, defensively. "I've snuck out while dad's at the lighthouse and Aunt Claire's at the café."

"That doesn't explain why you're out here," Henri said. "Were you hoping you could find whatever the smugglers left behind for yourself?" The accusation in her voice became stronger.

"No, that's not it." James shook his head vigorously. "I'd never do anything like that." It upset him that his new friend thought him the sort of person to break a promise. "I was thinking this morning, yesterday as well, that you struggled to get out of the tunnel the other day, and you're the smallest of us. If you only just managed to get through, the rest of us don't stand a chance. I snuck up here so I could dig out the entrance to the tunnel and make it easier for all of us."

"What do you mean?" Edward asked, stepping in before Henri's anger made her say something she would regret later.

"I took one of my dad's spades out there so I could make the hole bigger, big enough for all of us to fit through. I didn't go far into the tunnel, just far enough to be sure we'll be able to get through without any problems." He shifted his gaze from Edward to Henri then. "I thought if I did that today, the next time I can get out we'll be able to see if the tunnel does lead to Kierney's cave without us struggling just to get into the tunnel, which'll save us a load of time.

"I left the spade there in case we need it."

"Good thinking."

Henri reluctantly agreed with Edward's assessment of what James had done. Her anger faded to annoyance but didn't disappear entirely.

"So, when can we go looking for the cave?" she asked impatiently, tempted to suggest they go right then, regardless of the weather. She didn't, mostly because Elizabeth was urging them all to get moving again, rather than standing around in the rain, but also because she wasn't that stupid.

As eager as she was to go exploring, and to find somewhere that had been used by genuine smugglers — if only it had been pirates instead, she thought wistfully — she had enough sense to know that doing so just then was an invitation to either injury or death.

If it had just been a case of exploring some tunnels and caves, she wouldn't have hesitated, but at least part of their exploring would be done on a path that was not only open to the elements but a quarter of a mile above the sea. The chances of one of them falling were far too high for her to even suggest risking it.

"If I can get home without dad or Aunt Claire realising I've sneaked out," the look of cheeky confidence on his face suggested he was sure he could manage it, "then I might be able to get dad to let me out tomorrow. He doesn't often keep me grounded for long unless whatever I do involves Constable Lewis. He finds it too much of a pain keeping an eye on me. If he does let me out, we can see where the path leads, and if we need to come back at low tide to get to the cave." He had a feeling that that was what they were going to have to do, but he hoped not. They would have to get up very early to be there in time for low tide, far earlier than he liked to think about.

17

Brenda nudged the door open with her foot and entered the bedroom, a mug of hot chocolate in each hand and a biscuit tin dangling precariously from one finger.

Though it seemed that she must surely either drop the tin or spill the drinks, she made it to the table on Elizabeth's side of the bed, which was closest to the door, without incident.

She put down one of the gently steaming mugs, freeing up one hand, and then set the biscuit tin down next to it.

"Are you girls alright?" she asked as she made her way around the bed to give Henri her hot chocolate.

Henri nodded and reached eagerly for the mug that was now at her side. As far as she could tell, Brenda did nothing out of the ordinary to the hot chocolate she made, yet Henri liked it much more than she did that made by the housekeeper back home, even if it didn't have little marshmallows floating in it.

"We're fine, thank you," Elizabeth answered. Absently, she removed the lid from the biscuit tin, took out a couple of homemade cookies, and then passed the tin to her cousin.

"I hope you won't be too disturbed by the storm," Brenda said from the window, which she was checking to be sure it was securely fastened against the wind and the rain that raged outside the isolated farmhouse.

Elizabeth gave a quick smile. "I hope so too." She tried not to flinch as thunder crashed outside, seemingly right on top of them. She couldn't believe how bad the weather had been since they got there. It seemed to her that they had had more rain in the past week than they should have had all summer.

The rain that had soaked the teens as they walked back from the castle had gradually worsened, becoming a torrential downpour, the second of their holiday. Driven by the wind, which had increased in intensity to match the deluge, the rain had lashed into them almost painfully.

The wind and the rain were bad enough, but a few hours after they returned to the farm, thunder and lightning joined them, rocking the farmhouse and driving Lloyd and Brenda inside and away from their chores, which they had been struggling to finish.

"How long do you think the storm's going to last?" Henri asked of Elizabeth once Brenda had left. She was at the window, the curtain pulled back so she could look out.

She sipped at her hot chocolate while watching the storm for lightning strikes. She had never had an opportunity to see lightning properly, without it being either diminished by light pollution or obscured by buildings, and she was enjoying nature's show, though she did worry about how the chickens and the pigs would cope with the weather.

Elizabeth looked up in annoyance from her tablet, on which she was struggling to maintain an internet connection. The dongle Henri had bought didn't work well with the weather so bad.

"How am I supposed to know?" she asked. Jabbing a finger at the screen of her tablet, she tried once more to send the message she had written. "Do I look like a weather girl?"

Henri was tempted to say that yes, she often did look like a weather girl, but she resisted, knowing it would only make Elizabeth more irritable than she already was. Instead, she shrugged and said, "I only asked. It'll be finished by morning, won't it?"

"I hope so." Elizabeth had no idea how long such a storm might last. It had already been going for almost half the day with no sign of abating. She thought it must at least ease by morning, she couldn't see how it could keep up its current intensity until then, but she didn't feel confident that it would.

Not in the least satisfied with her cousin's response, Henri watched the storm until she finished her hot chocolate, and then she returned to the bed.

THE HOPED-FOR END TO the storm came in the early hours of the morning.

The thunder and lightning died away gradually during the night, but the rain persisted. It lashed down for hour after hour, until it stopped abruptly, as though someone had turned off a tap.

The end of the rain came with a silence that was so sudden and complete that it woke Henri from her deep sleep.

It took her a few moments to realise what it was that had woken her and when she did, she slipped from under the duvet, moving as quietly and carefully as she could to avoid waking Elizabeth, and crossed to the window.

It was still dark. A lightening of the sky as the moon tried to shine through the battered remnants of the storm clouds allowed her to see that the rain had stopped, but since she couldn't make out anything more of the outside, she returned to bed.

Despite the care she took not to disturb her cousin, Henri had no sooner settled her head on the pillow than Elizabeth rolled over.

"Is the storm finished?" she asked in a sleepy voice.

"Looks like it," Henri said in a voice that was as quiet and sleep-filled as her cousin's.

Neither girl spoke again, instead, they settled down to get what sleep they could in the last few hours of the night.

18

Henri was struggling through the thick mud of the yard on her way back to the house with the eggs she had collected when a car pulled up to the gate. She barely had a chance to register its arrival before the passenger door flew open and James almost catapulted into sight.

"Morning," Henri called out, surprised by the earliness of James' arrival. She hadn't long finished her breakfast and hadn't expected to see him for at least another hour, if he was allowed to leave the house at all.

She returned her attention to the ground at her feet almost immediately. She wasn't concerned about falling over and getting herself muddy, though she didn't fancy having to clean herself up and pick out a new outfit after already having had a wash. What she was concerned about was breaking the eggs in her basket.

She didn't like to think what Lloyd would say if she returned to the house with nothing but a mass of broken shells and a messy basket. Nothing nice, she was sure.

"Morning. Bye," James called back over his shoulder to Claire, who was behind the wheel of the car. "You don't have to worry about picking me up, I'll walk home later." He shut the door with a bang and made his way around the car to the gate, swinging his bag up onto his shoulder as he went.

He slipped through the gate and hurried over to Henri, wishing with every squelching step that he had thought to put on his wellington boots rather than his trainers, which he was in danger of losing to the mud.

"How come you're here so early?" Henri asked as the two of them made their way around the side of the house to the kitchen door.

James smiled. "I want as much time for exploring as possible. Claire persuaded dad to let me come out today, so I thought I'd get here as early as I can. Who knows how long it's going to take us to follow Kierney's path. It might not lead straight from the top of the cliff to either the beach or the cave, it could go all over the place."

"Do you think that's likely?" Henri hoped not. If the path did go all over the place, it might prove too lengthy for them to get anywhere before they had to turn around to get back to the farm in time for dinner.

"Not really. I doubt Kierney would have used a path that takes ages. He'd have wanted to get things done as quickly as possible." Though he said that confidently, James wasn't sure and was basing it on how he would have operated if he were a smuggler who had to be constantly on the alert for the customs people.

"You'd better think again, James Allen, if you think you're coming into my clean kitchen with those muddy trainers on," Brenda said sharply as he was about to step over the threshold. "If you leave so much as a single footprint on my floor, you'll be cleaning it up." She reached past James, who stopped abruptly just outside the back door so he could slip his trainers off, to take the basket from Henri. "Thank you, dear. Have you fed them yet?"

Henri nodded. "Yes, I fed them first, then got the eggs while they were at the feed. I got them water as well."

"Good girl. You'd better go and get yourself sorted then if you're going off somewhere."

THE WALK TO THE TUNNEL Henri had found took longer than it should, thanks mostly to the sogginess of the ground, which had become almost like a quagmire after soaking up so much rain during the night.

Elizabeth wanted to walk along the road, which was solid, and unaffected by the rain, but James pointed out that it wouldn't save them either time or effort. The distance from the road to the tunnel was nearly the same as that from the farm to the tunnel, so they would still have to walk almost a mile across waterlogged country.

James also pointed out that Elizabeth was the only one of them who didn't have to worry about the soggy ground. Since she was almost the same size as Brenda, she had been able to borrow a pair of wellington boots to keep her feet dry, while the rest of them were stuck wearing trainers that were going to need a lot of cleaning after their day's adventuring.

When they reached the tunnel, Elizabeth happily obeyed James' advice to stay back out of the way while he checked the entrance to the tunnel, to make sure the excavations he had made the previous day hadn't been disturbed by the storm.

"It's alright, it looks like it's safe. The storm didn't damage it or anything," James said after a minute or so of poking and prodding at the ground around the hole with the spade he had left there. "Pass me one of the torches."

Edward checked the torch was working before he passed it over, even though he knew the batteries in it, like the torch itself, were brand new. He then watched James climb down into the tunnel, thinking that as the eldest, he should have been the one to go first. He thought the same thing when Henri followed James into the hole, but she was gone before he could stop her.

"Go on, you next," he said to Elizabeth. Since he wasn't leading the group, he thought it best if he brought up the rear. That way he was best positioned to react if anything happened.

Elizabeth eyed the hole distastefully and shook her head. "I think one of us should stay here, so they can go for help if anything goes wrong."

"You won't know if anything goes wrong, though," Edward pointed out. "We won't be in sight, and you probably won't be able to hear us. We won't be able to get you on your mobile either, we can't get a signal out here."

"If you haven't come back in a couple of hours, I'll assume something's wrong and go for help," Elizabeth said. It wasn't that she was scared of the tunnel, or the path that lay beyond it — at least that was what she told herself — she just thought it sensible to have someone stay behind, someone who could say where the others had gone if anything prevented them returning.

Edward considered what his sister had said for a few moments and then nodded in agreement. He could see that Elizabeth didn't want to go exploring and was only there because he and Henri were, but he could also see the sense in what she had said.

"Okay, you stay here. I just hope you don't get too bored or anything." He was about to enter the hole so he could catch up to the other two, who he hoped had waited for him, when he thought of something and turned back. "You'd better wait until mid-afternoon before going for help. We don't know how long it's going to take us to get to the end of the path and come back, let alone explore if we do find the cave."

Elizabeth nodded, though she wasn't happy with the thought of waiting so long to go for help if they didn't come back. Mid-afternoon was six hours away, and a lot of things could happen in that time, most of them bad. Any delay in getting help could prove serious, perhaps even fatal.

The moment her brother was out of sight, her mind began to list the things that could occur, starting with the merely awful and quickly building towards the cataclysmic.

Edward caught up with Henri and James at the far end of the tunnel, which was shorter than he had expected. In a straight line, he figured it would have run for no more than about thirty metres, though because of the twists and turns it took it was closer to half again as long.

"Where's Lizzie?" Henri asked when she saw that Edward was alone in the light from the torches she and James held.

"She's not coming. She's decided that one of us should stay up top in case of trouble," Edward said. "She plans on getting help if anything happens to us or we're not back by mid-afternoon. Since we don't know how long it's going to take us to find the cave, if it exists, I think we'd better get going." He turned off his torch as he followed the other two out of the tunnel and into the open air to start along the narrow path that provided a way down the almost sheer face of the cliff.

The path, which appeared to be natural in origin, was just about wide enough for an adult to manoeuvre along, which meant it was big enough to give the teens some safety, though not much.

They moved with as much care and caution as they could, aware that the slightest misstep would see them tumble to the surf below, with no way to stop themselves before they reached it.

"Is that something down there?"

The trio were still fifty or so metres above the narrow strip of land that had been exposed by the low tide, which was on its way back in but hadn't yet fully returned, when James stopped. Being at the front of the group, he had an unobscured view of what lay ahead and below them, whereas Henri and Edward had to move with extreme caution to get into a position where they could see past James to what he had spotted.

Thankfully, though not tall for his age, Edward was tall enough to see over the other two because of his position at the rear of the trio, which meant he was higher on the path.

"They look like boxes," he said after studying the distant objects for a few moments.

"That's what I thought."

Eager to find out exactly what it was they could see, James set off again, hurrying down the narrow path at an unsafe speed.

He nearly slipped a couple of times but made it unharmed to the end of the path, where he discovered the tide had come in far enough for the narrow beach to be under a couple of inches of water.

Some of the boxes had been lifted by the water, while others remained stuck where they were. How long it would be before the last of the boxes floated free was hard to tell. It was unlikely to be long, though, and realising that James stepped into the water.

His feet were immediately soaked by the incoming tide, which washed over his trainers, but he ignored that and focused on discovering what was in the boxes. He hoped it was something either interesting or valuable, preferably both.

Henri followed James without hesitation, as unconcerned by the sudden soaking of her feet as he was.

"Where do you think they came from?" she asked upon reaching the first of the boxes, which James was already working to open, a task made difficult by how wet it.

"They must have come from a boat," James said. "Probably got washed overboard during the storm. Dad said some boats got in trouble and had to be helped by the lifeboat guys from the mainland. When there's a really bad storm, he has to stay at the lighthouse to make sure nothing goes wrong and help gets to whoever needs it," he explained upon seeing the curious look on Henri's face. "There's nothing on any of these to say what boat they're from, though, or where they were being taken, or even what's in them." He was disappointed by the lack of information.

"That's weird, isn't it?" Henri said.

"It's a little weird," Edward said from the path. "I'd expect the boxes to be like those on a delivery van, with shipping labels or something to identify them, so people at least know where they're going, if not what's in them." The lack of labels or other information pushed him to abandon his decision to keep his feet dry and he stepped off the path to wade through the deepening water to the other two.

When the sodden box finally succumbed to James' efforts to open it, it revealed itself to be filled with cigarettes, carton after carton of them. There were thousands of cigarettes in total, the three teens estimated. Enough to keep even the biggest of chain-smokers supplied for months, if not a whole year.

After exchanging matching looks of disappointment, Henri and James moved on to the next box, forcing their way through the incoming tide. They hoped they would find something other than cigarettes this time, something that might be of interest or value to them.

They were out of luck.

They had more success with the third box they checked. Inside it, sealed in their boxes, were thousands, if not tens of thousands of pounds worth of mobile phones. The latest models, from a variety of companies.

The full value of the box's contents could only be guessed at by the teens, but it was easily enough that Edward and Henri, who were used to money, found it amazing to be confronted by such a valuable collection of items.

Something bumped against Henri's leg as she and James waded towards the next box causing her a moment's panic. She relaxed when she looked down and saw that it was a bottle of alcohol, clearly from one of the boxes that had been broken open during their journey through the rocks. She hadn't noticed them before but at least a dozen bottles were floating amongst the lost cargo.

"I think we'd better get out of here and call the police," Edward called out to the other two, stopping them before they could reach the next box.

"Why?" James couldn't think of a reason for calling the police, but he could see the sense in getting out of there. The tide had risen to the point where it was approaching their knees and was still coming in. How much farther it would rise, he couldn't be sure, but they would soon be in danger of having their feet swept out from under them, and that was something they wanted to avoid.

Edward didn't answer James until the three of them were out of the surf and safely back on the path to the top of the cliff.

"We need to call the police," he said, "because I think someone is using the cave we were looking for for smuggling, like Kierney did back in the eighteen-hundreds."

James looked at Edward dubiously. He liked the idea that there might still be smugglers in operation, and that they might be repeating history by using the old cave, but he couldn't quite believe it.

"There aren't any smugglers anymore, just like there aren't pirates anymore. It's a shame, I'd like there to be, but there aren't."

"There are," Edward said. "I guess you don't read the papers much or watch the news." He wasn't big on paying attention to the news either, but it was always on in his parents' house, so he couldn't miss it. "If anything, there's more smugglers now than there were in the eighteen-hundreds. They smuggle just about anything: cigarettes, tobacco, alcohol, mobile phones and other electrical goods stolen abroad, fake fashion-label clothes. Anything they can make money on, even people. You hear about pirates as well, off the coast of Africa. They hijack boats and hold them for ransom. All of this," he gestured at the boxes that bobbed on the tide, "looks like the kind of stuff smugglers would deal in. Plus, there's part of a boat down there, a small one, the sort that might be able to get through the rocks to the cave.

"We need to tell the police, so they can check it out."

James was reluctant to reveal his exploring to Constable Lewis, sure that his father would be told, and he would then get into trouble for putting himself at risk, but he knew Edward was right. He didn't have a clue about modern-day smugglers or African pirates, and he wasn't convinced that if they existed, they were using the island, but if a boat had gone down in the storm, a search would have to be made for survivors by the coastguard from the mainland.

Any cargo that had been lost by a boat that had suffered in the storm would have to be recovered as well, if possible. James knew from his father just how little it took for an object to become a hazard to boats.

Big ships would likely run down any lost cargo without even noticing it, but a smaller boat could end up with damage to either hull or engine if they struck something.

Henri hovered between the two boys, both physically and mentally. Physically, she stood in the middle of the trio, a short distance from where the incoming tide encroached on the cliff path. Mentally, she wasn't sure what to make of the situation.

She knew a little about modern-day smuggling — like Edward's parents, her mum and dad had the news on almost constantly, so she couldn't help seeing and hearing what was going on in the world, even if she wasn't always interested in it — but found it hard to believe that they might have stumbled on anything to do with it, though the idea did excite her.

The journey to the top of the cliff took less time than the descent, both because they were more familiar with the path and because Edward moved quicker. He wanted to get somewhere he could receive a signal on his phone, so he could call Constable Lewis and report what they had discovered.

Barely half an hour after beginning their ascent, they were out of the hole under the gorse bush, much to the relief of Elizabeth, and heading for the farm.

19

Constable Lewis took his time responding to the phone call from Edward.

Almost an hour passed from the time of the call before he arrived at the farm. Time enough for Edward to tell Brenda and Lloyd where he, Henri, Elizabeth, and James had gone, what they had seen, and why they had called Constable Lewis. Time enough also for them to change into dry clothes — James had borrowed some from Edward, though they didn't fit him well — and have a cup of tea to warm themselves up.

Neither Brenda nor Lloyd was happy when they heard what their charges had been up to and the risks they had taken. The risks were bad enough, but both Brenda and Lloyd thought it worse that the teens had not given any hint of where they were going in the note they had left that morning. If anything had happened, nobody would have had any idea where to find them.

When he finally arrived at the farm, Constable Lewis bustled into the kitchen with the air of someone who had been called away from the greatest of emergencies to deal with a cat up a tree.

It was clear from the first moment that he wasn't pleased to have been called out to the farm by children. It was an opinion that became more obvious when he saw James Allen seated at the kitchen table.

After a scowl in James' direction, he addressed himself to Edward, "I assume it was you who called me. Edward Bligh, correct?"

Edward nodded and said, "Yes."

Without invitation, Lewis took a seat. He set his helmet down in the middle of the table and then took out a small notebook and a pen. He scribbled for a moment to be sure the pen was working, and only when he was satisfied did, he return his attention to Edward.

"Before we get to the reason for your call to the station," he said, "I need to take down a few details, starting with your full name. I'll need the names of the girls as well." He indicated Elizabeth and Henri with his pen.

"Is that necessary?" Brenda asked. "You're here because the kids found what might have been a boat caught in the storm. Surely you should be getting those details, so you can call in the coastguard to check for survivors."

Lewis hid his annoyance as best he could as he turned to Brenda. "I am aware of the reason I was called out here, and I'll deal with it shortly. I need the names of these three, though, so I can include them in the report I'll have to make out. Your full name, please," he said to Edward.

"You're not really going to waste time with this nonsense, are you?" Brenda asked without giving Edward a chance to respond to the question put to him.

Stiffly, as though mortally offended, Lewis drew himself up in his seat and said, with as much dignity as he could muster, "This is not nonsense, this is police business, and there are procedures to be followed. I'll thank you not to talk down about the work I do protecting this island and its citizens."

Brenda snorted at that, making it clear what she thought of Lewis' pronouncement.

Lloyd got to his feet quickly to forestall Lewis, who was visibly bristling, from saying something he would regret later. "You can get the kids' names another time," he said firmly, his tone brooking no argument. "If a boat's run afoul of last night's storm, we need to check it out now. I'll go with you."

The decisiveness in Lloyd's voice overwhelmed Lewis and left him with no choice but to go along as hurried preparations were made.

It took a short while to organise things to Lloyd's satisfaction, and then Edward, Elizabeth, Henri, and James led Lloyd and Lewis across the moor to the tunnel they had found and the path that lay beyond it.

"How the hell am I supposed to fit through there?" Lewis wanted to know when he saw the hole in the ground he had been brought to.

"Suck in your gut," James told him with a cheeky grin before skipping quickly out of the way to avoid being clipped around the ear.

"Once you get through the entrance, it widens out," Edward said. "You should be alright." He started forward to lead the way but was stopped by Lloyd's hand on his arm.

"No, you don't," Lloyd said. "It's bad enough you kids went down there without an adult this morning. I'm not going to let you go down there again."

"You need us to show you the way, though," Henri said. Ducking under Lloyd's arm, she all but dived into the hole.

James followed Henri without hesitation, just managing to avoid Lloyd's fingers as he sought to stop him.

Lloyd went next, so he could stop the impetuous teens before they went too far. As he climbed down into the hole he wondered if he was being led on a wild goose chase, or if there really was evidence of a wreck to be found at the end of the path. He couldn't decide which he preferred; a wild goose chase would be annoying, but a wreck would mean a search would have to be made for survivors, and this long after the storm, the chances of anyone still being alive were slim.

Edward, ignoring the injunction from Lewis against doing so, slipped easily through the hole once Lloyd was out of the way.

Lewis was the last of them into the tunnel, Elizabeth again deciding not to descend into the cliff, and when he reached the others, his uniform gave mute evidence of the struggle it had been for him to get that far. He was covered in dirt, and several tears revealed that he had caught himself on the gorse bush that protected the entrance.

"You made it through then," James said, grinning in the light from the torch he was carrying. The state of Lewis' uniform amused him, and he couldn't help thinking that whatever else happened, the day had been worth it simply to see the constable in such a mess.

Lewis scowled fiercely and looked as though he was going to say something sharp to James when Lloyd spoke.

"Which way now?" He shone the torch he held around the tunnel and saw there were no side tunnels or deviations, it only went in one direction. He also saw that the roof of the tunnel got lower further on, meaning he was going to have to be careful. He was the tallest one there, and the one most likely to hit their head if the tunnel got too low, which he didn't fancy doing.

"Just follow the tunnel," Edward said. "It doesn't go far. After a few twists and turns, it comes out on the path that leads down to the base of the cliff."

"Okay, let's get this done," Lloyd said, indicating that Henri and James should move off. He would have preferred to move ahead of the teens, so he could lead the way in case they encountered any trouble, but it was obvious there wasn't enough space, and they would all have to stay in the order in which they had entered the tunnel.

The teens had no problem, either with the tunnel or the path down the face of the cliff. Not only were they familiar with the route, or at least not strangers to it, they were more sure-footed than either of the adults, and they had the advantage of there being more space for them because of their smaller sizes.

The adults were not so fortunate. Lloyd had to walk bent over for almost half the tunnel to avoid bumping his head, and after he made it through there he struggled with the path. The shifting of small stones under his feet caused problems for his balance, which wasn't what it had been when he was younger.

Lewis also struggled, but for him, it was his waistline rather than his height that caused him problems. He made it through the tunnel okay after his struggle with the entrance, but he found the path that led down the cliff too narrow for a heavy-set person like himself.

Despite the difficulties of the descent, they all made it to the point where the path disappeared under the water without injury or incident.

When they did, they discovered that aside from one box, the cargo and the floating debris was gone.

"Well, where's the wrecked boat you say you saw?" Lewis demanded, almost knocking the others off the path and into the water as he tried to get past them to get a better look at the mostly empty sea.

Edward was surprised by the disappearance of what he, Henri, and James had seen that morning, but not so much that he missed the mistake Lewis had made.

"I never said I saw a wrecked boat. I said I saw some wreckage that looked like it came from a damaged boat and some cargo that must have been lost overboard during the storm."

"Okay, well, there's no sign of your damaged boat here, and other than that one box, no sign of the cargo you say was here. Is this your idea of a joke, bringing me out here on a wild-goose chase?" Lewis looked far from pleased by the thought.

"Of course not," Edward said quickly. He realised the constable didn't know him, but it still annoyed him that someone would think him the sort of person to play a joke like that. He had played the occasional joke in the past, but never on an adult, and certainly not of the sort he was being accused of then.

Out the corner of his eye, he saw Henri on the verge of exploding at Lewis, almost certainly with a tirade that would get her in trouble, while James, who was clearly used to being disbelieved, contented himself with a disgusted shake of his head.

"Why on earth would I do something like that?" Edward wanted to know. "I don't know what happened to it all, but there was getting on for a dozen boxes here earlier, all of them at least as big as that one. They had cigarettes, tobacco, alcohol, and mobile phones in them. There were pieces of a small boat here as well. I'm no expert, but it looked like they were from a speedboat or something like that."

"Well. it can't have all been carried off by the tide," Lloyd said, looking around with an experienced eye. He was a farmer by tradition and experience but living on a small island he couldn't help but know a little about tides too. "It's come in, not gone out. If anything, there should be more stuff here."

"Maybe the smugglers collected their lost cargo, and the bits of their boat, to stop people finding out they're using Kierney's old smuggling cave," James said offering his opinion on what had happened.

"What on earth are you talking about?" Lewis wanted to know. "Smugglers. Kierney's smuggling cave." He shook his head. "This is your wild imagination at work, isn't it. There aren't any smugglers here, and no one's ever found Kierney's cave. No one's even proved it ever existed. It's either that or you're having a laugh at my expense, and you've persuaded these two, and Elizabeth Bligh, to go along with it."

James tried hard to tell Lewis that it was not a joke and that he wasn't involved with Edward, Henri, and Elizabeth in an attempt to make a fool of him.

Edward also tried to reassure Lewis that he was not the subject of a prank.

Henri, however, clenched her fists and fought the urge to lash out angrily. She was not by nature a violent person, but if there was one thing that always got her riled up, it was being accused of lying.

Lewis paid no attention to the teens, though. Instead, he turned and started back up the path to the clifftop, moving as quickly as he could on the narrow trail. His pace and demeanour made it clear that he had no interest in hearing what James and his friends had to say, and even less interest in investigating to see if they had told him the truth.

Lloyd was silent for several long moments as he watched Lewis and then he turned to the teens. "If he doesn't think there's anything that can be done here, there's no point in us sticking around," he said, concealing his disappointment in the constable's reaction to the situation. "We'd better go back up and get ourselves on safe ground."

20

Brenda looked quizzically at her husband when he returned with the teens.

"What happened?" she asked as she bustled about the kitchen, putting the kettle on, and preparing a teapot along with cups and mugs for all of them. "Lewis came back a short while ago, didn't say anything to me, just muttered something about jokes, smugglers, and wasting his time. He didn't even answer me when I asked if you were all okay and on your way back; he just got in his car and drove away."

Lloyd sat heavily in the scarred and worn chair he had used for the past five decades. He was used to working hard and being active, but the descent and ascent of the cliff trail was a different kind of labour to what he was accustomed to, and it had taken it out of him.

"The things the kids saw this morning were gone by the time we got there," he said after allowing himself a moment to get his breath back. "All there was, was one box, too far away to see what was in it, and a few small bits of flotsam — they could have been anything. Lewis decided it was a prank, thought up by James to mess with him."

James looked mortally offended by the notion that he would do such a thing.

"I don't think the situation was helped by James deciding that what they had found belonged to smugglers, and the smugglers had come back to retrieve their lost cargo, and that was why it was no longer there."

Brenda looked from her husband to James. "Smugglers?" she said in a tone of disbelief. "Are you sure this wasn't a prank?" When James nodded vehemently, she went on, "What on Earth would make you think of smugglers? You must have known Lewis would have a hard time believing you with the evidence gone. Talking about smugglers was only going to make it harder for him to believe you.

"You're lucky he didn't arrest you for wasting his time."

James found his voice then. "If he'd arrested me, he'd have had to arrest all of us. That's way too much paperwork for him. Besides, he wouldn't dare arrest someone related to the baron, that'd cause too much trouble for him."

"That's true enough," Brenda agreed. She knew as well as anyone how much Lewis would like to do something to curb the island's chief troublemaker, but she also knew he had an aversion to work, especially the form-filling variety, and trouble. That was why he continued to be the constable of a small island, rather than getting a transfer to somewhere where he would have better promotion prospects. "If you weren't all playing a prank on Lewis, and you did see boxes and part of a damaged boat, and they're not there now, what happened to it all? Surely the tide didn't take it away."

Lloyd shook his head. "No, the tide won't be going out for another couple of hours. If it was going to do anything, it would have brought more stuff in, not taken it away."

"Then what happened to it?"

"Since I didn't see the items in the first place, I can't even begin to guess," Lloyd said. He wasn't happy about that, he liked a nice, orderly life where he knew what was going on, not mysteries, like things disappearing without an explanation.

"You do believe us, don't you?" Henri asked of Lloyd. "We wouldn't have lied about something like that."

"Of course, dear," Brenda answered for her husband. "We know that. It's just a bit odd that it all disappeared." She set about pouring out the tea then.

"I still say the smugglers took it all away, so they wouldn't get caught," James said.

"How, though?" Lloyd asked. "Assuming you're right and what you saw this morning came from smugglers, they couldn't have taken it all away. There wasn't time for them to get another boat there to collect everything you said you saw, and it would have been impossible for them to carry something the size of the box I saw up the path and through that bit of tunnel.

"Even if it were possible, there wasn't time for them to get rid of everything. They'd have still been there when we arrived."

James had to think about that for a few moments before he came up with an answer.

"They must have been hiding in the cave while we were there," he said. "They must have been grabbing their cargo when we came. When they heard us, they hid in the cave. Then, once we left, they came back out and got everything they could — maybe the water was too deep for them to get the last box or something." He nodded, as if in agreement with his own words. "They must be using the cave for storage like Kierney did in the eighteen-hundreds, and either waiting there for high tide so they can leave again in another boat, or they have another way out of the cave.

"Maybe they know where the entrance to the tunnel is hidden in Kierney's house," he said as the idea occurred to him.

21

James closed the book he had been reading and tossed it onto the table with the others.

"Nothing," he said in disgust. "Absolutely nothing." He hadn't expected to find anything since he had been through the books before, but he had hoped he might previously have missed something.

"Same here," Henri said with a sigh of irritation, closing her book. "They all say the tunnels and the cave are there, and that Kierney's house is built over the main entrance to the tunnels, but according to the books, no one has ever seen them. A couple of people have said they've seen a cave from a distance while out on the water, apparently, but none of them could get close enough, because of the rocks, to say for definite it was Kierney's cave."

Edward said nothing, he simply got to his feet so he could begin replacing the books they had been reading, all of which were to do with either the island and its history or smuggling in that area during the eighteen-hundreds. He wasn't sure he was putting them back where they had come from, but he didn't suppose that mattered much. As far as he could tell, the library was seldom used and there was no real organisation to its shelves.

"What do we do now?" Henri asked. It hadn't been her idea to come to the library, she had accepted James' word that he had read every relevant book in the library and found nothing to help them locate the hidden tunnel, or to help them pinpoint the exact location of the cave.

To her mind, since they couldn't find either the cave or the tunnel through the books in the library, the only thing they could do was explore. She was sure that if they went back to the burnt-out house and spent enough time exploring, they would find what they were looking for.

James shrugged, as lost for ideas as Henri. "It's too late to go back out there now. I say we go see if Aunt Claire will give us some free drinks."

"Sounds good..."

"I think I've got something," Elizabeth interrupted Henri. She set the book she was reading down and leant over it, her finger marking the passage she had found. "According to this, Solomon Kierney managed some last words before he died. He told the customs officers who shot him that they would never find the entrance, that the fire would protect his secret."

"Not very helpful," Edward remarked. "Having seen the house, and read all of this, he must have been trying to warn them that if they tried searching for the entrance to the tunnel, they'd set off his boobytrap and burn the house down."

"Maybe." Elizabeth was not as certain as her brother. "I think we should speak to Father Jacobs about it."

"...CLEANED IT ALL UP, so don't worry...."

Edward, Elizabeth, Henri, and James all knew it was rude to eavesdrop on someone else's conversation, but they couldn't help stopping to listen when they heard the low voice. The speaker was around the corner from them, so they couldn't tell who it was, but there was something about the voice, and what it was saying, and especially the way the speaker clearly didn't want to be overheard, that made them ignore the rudeness of what they were doing and continue listening.

"I said don't worry. I got it before they got back there. And I just heard the local plod in the pub; he thinks the kids were winding him up, so he's not going to be any trouble. Besides, he's an idiot."

There was silence for several long moments and then the voice started up again.

"We lost about a third of the cargo, the water wrecked it. We're going to have to replace it."

Another pause.

"I know it's risky, but we don't have a choice, we've got people waiting for the stuff."

The teens shared significant looks as they listened to the one-sided conversation going on around the corner. They were all thinking the same thing, that they were right about the smugglers using the old cave, and that one of them was just a few feet away.

"Can you get another boat in time for tonight or not?"

The sound of heavy footsteps receding indicated the speaker was moving away, and his voice faded slowly, becoming harder to hear, as he did so.

"We need to know who he is," James said in a quiet voice, not wanting to be heard by the smuggler, who knew about them, though he didn't know how.

Edward reached out to pull James back. "You can't go out there. If he sees you, who knows what he'll do."

"We have to know who he is, so we can tell Lewis." James was determined to prove he hadn't been playing a prank that morning and oblivious to the irony that if he hadn't played so many pranks over the years, he wouldn't have been thought to be playing one then. With a sudden jerk, he pulled himself free from Edward's grip and hurried around the corner.

His hopes of identifying the smuggler and clearing his reputation were quickly dashed. The short street was empty. Seeing that, he ran for the far end, barely a hundred yards away, so he could look up and down the next street. He saw three people, but immediately discounted one of them because it was a woman, and the voice they had heard had belonged to a man.

"Who is it?" Henri asked, stopping at James' side. She scrutinised the two men she could see, but they were both walking away from her, and she doubted she would have been able to identify them even if she could see more than just the backs of their heads.

She didn't know any of the island's residents, other than Brenda, Lloyd, and James, and possibly Father Jacobs, well enough to recognise them at a distance, especially from behind.

James did know most of the island's residents well enough to recognise them. He still needed a few moments before he was willing to commit himself, though.

"It's Sean Patricks," he said finally.

"Are you sure?" Edward asked. He hadn't previously been certain that the lost cargo they had found belonged to smugglers, but he was now. The overheard phone conversation had convinced him. He wasn't about to go to the police and accuse someone of being a smuggler, however, not unless James was certain he had the right person. After the way Lewis had reacted to the suggestion that someone might be using the island for smuggling, Edward was sure it was going to take some work to convince him.

"Yes," James said with a confident nod. "The guy on the right is Mr Elroy. It can't be him because he used to be a fisherman, working the boats out of the harbour, and he had to give it up after an accident. I don't know what happened, something to do with him getting trapped in a net one day, I heard, but he's missing two fingers on his right hand, and the top part of another. Plus, he's got a bad knee and a major limp, as you can see. He has difficulty going up and down stairs most days, so..."

"So, he'd have a lot of difficulty moving around in tunnels through a cliff, and a lot more getting all that stuff we saw out of the surf," Edward concluded.

James nodded. "I should have guessed Patricks is the smuggler. It's obvious now I think about it. He's never made himself a part of the island. He's loaded apparently, but no one knows where he got his money, no one I know anyway, and he built a house on the cliff not far from Kierney's house."

"How come we didn't see it?" Henri asked.

Aside from the ruin of Kierney's house, and the road to the castle, they hadn't seen so much as a hint of anything manmade while they were trying to find the cave used by Kierney.

"He had a bunch of trees planted all around his house," James said. "He wanted privacy apparently, even though there's just about never anyone close enough to see the place. You can see it from the water, from what I've heard, but not from the land, not unless you follow the drive he had built from the road. And you can't even see that from a distance."

They hadn't even seen it up close when they walked back along the road from the castle, Henri thought.

"Come on." James turned and strode off abruptly, leaving the others to stare after him, with no clue where he was going or why.

James was walking so quickly that the cousins didn't catch up to him until he was at the door of the island's tiny police station.

He slipped through the door just as they reached him, giving them no time to stop him, and leaving them with no choice about whether to tell Constable Lewis about the phone call they had overheard, or their suspicions about Sean Patricks.

"What are you doing here?" Lewis asked sharply when he saw who had entered the station. "Come to annoy me some more? Have you decided that aliens are responsible for your disappearing cargo now, or maybe sea monsters?"

"Neither, but I am here about the stuff we found this morning," James said, ignoring the sarcasm in Lewis' voice. He wasn't keen on being there, he had been taken to the police station too many times when he was in trouble to want to be there voluntarily, but he was determined to clear his name.

"I'm not interested," Lewis said. "I went with you this morning, despite my misgivings, but there was nothing to see. I doubt there ever was, aside from that one box. If you want to continue with this story about smugglers, I'll have to have words with your father." It was clear he intended that as a threat. "You won't like that."

"I'm not playing a prank," James said insistently. "There really was all that stuff at the end of the path we found, and it really was taken away by the smugglers. And we know who they are, one of them at least. We overheard him just now, talking to one of his accomplices."

"Really. Go on then, who is this smuggler?" Lewis asked. He made a pretence of being interested, but all the teens could tell he was only doing so because he figured listening was the quickest way to get rid of them.

"Patricks. Sean Patricks is the smuggler," James said. "We heard him on the phone talking about clearing everything up before we got back with you and Mr B."

"Mr Patricks is a successful businessman, and very rich. Why would he have anything to do with smuggling?" Lewis wanted to know.

"We've only got his word for it that he's a successful businessman," James said. "Nobody knows what his business is supposed to be. All we know is he's got money, and he could have got that from smuggling."

Lewis put down his mug and leant forward to fix James with a hard look. "If I were you, I would be very careful about making unfounded accusations, especially against someone like Mr Patricks. From the little I know of him, he wouldn't take kindly to being accused of breaking the law, and the fact that you're a kid wouldn't stop him suing you."

"But he is one of the smugglers," James insisted, his voice rising with indignation at not being believed. "We heard him, didn't we?" He turned to his friends for support.

Elizabeth gave every indication of wanting to be left out of things, but Henri nodded in agreement, and Edward felt compelled to say, "We definitely heard someone speaking on a phone. He said he managed to get everything back, but it was wrecked and would have to be replaced. He also said he heard you in the pub, and that you won't be any trouble because you're an idiot and think we were winding you up."

That was the last straw for Lewis.

"Get out," he ordered sharply, his face red with anger. He followed them to the door, all but chasing them out of the station, and slammed it shut behind them. He then locked it to keep them from coming back in and annoying him further.

"I don't think you should have told him he'd been called an idiot," Elizabeth told her brother.

The teens stood in the street outside the station for almost a minute, too stunned by their sudden eviction to say or do anything.

22

The moment the door opened to reveal James' father, Edward, Elizabeth, and Henri knew that their plans for the day were about to change.

"Is James in?" Henri asked, hoping her concerns were unfounded.

"Yes, but he's not coming out," Paul Allen said.

"Why not? Is he alright?"

"Aside from being grounded, yes."

Henri was tempted to ask why James was grounded, but she was sure she already knew, so instead, she asked, "How long is he grounded for? Will he be allowed out tomorrow?"

"No, he won't be out tomorrow. After yesterday, he'll be lucky if he gets out of the house before the end of the summer." Paul Allen glared at the cousins, as though they were the reason his son was in trouble, even though they all knew that James was in trouble more often than he was out of it.

"Why didn't he call to say he's been grounded?" Henri asked, put out that they had gone there when it wasn't necessary.

"Because I've taken his mobile away, and he's not allowed to use the house phone, except for emergencies. He's being punished," Paul Allen said, "so he's not allowed any contact with his friends." His tone conveyed what he thought of his son's friends — nothing complimentary.

He closed the door with a bang then, leaving the cousins, who were taken aback by his brusque manner, on the doorstep, feeling much the same as they had the previous day when Lewis locked them out of the police station.

They stood there for several long moments, not sure what to do, and then turned away to try and find something to do.

It was too late for them to go over to the mainland; they had missed the ferry by over an hour. None of them fancied going back to the farm, where their choices would be between boredom and unwelcome labour, and Blighton held no interest for them, given its lack of entertainment possibilities.

Unfortunately, with those possibilities eliminated, they only had a couple of options available to them. They could either go out to the castle or they could explore more of the island.

Henri didn't mind what they did, she just didn't want to sit around on a sunny day.

Elizabeth wasn't enthusiastic about either choice, she had done as much exploring as she could handle, for the time being at least, and the castle was too far away to get to easily.

Edward was left with the deciding vote on what they would do, but he couldn't make up his mind. He fancied doing something different, but nothing different came to mind.

Their aimless meandering, while they tried to decide what to do, led them, almost inevitably, to the harbour. There was nothing for them to do there, just like elsewhere in Blighton, but the sunshine was unobscured, and there were the comings and goings on the water, both of man and bird, to watch.

"Hello, you three."

The greeting caught Edward, Elizabeth, and Henri all by surprise as they strolled towards the rocks that separated the harbour from the narrow strip of sand that passed for a beach.

Almost in unison, they spun around to see who the voice belonged to. Why they should react so nervously to a simple greeting, none of them could have said, but they relaxed when they saw that the speaker was Father Jacobs, who looked uncomfortably warm in his black priestly attire.

"Sorry, I didn't mean to startle you," he apologised.

"It's okay, Father," Edward said, recovering from his momentary surprise. "I guess we were lost in our thoughts."

"It is a lovely day for letting your mind drift and go wherever it wants to," Father Jacobs remarked, lifting his eyes briefly to the almost cloudless blue sky overhead. "Where's James? I would have thought he'd be out here with you, enjoying the sunshine."

"He's been grounded again," Henri said unhappily.

"What's he done this time?" Father Jacobs asked, torn between amusement and annoyance that his young friend was once more in trouble.

"Nothing, nothing wrong at least. It's all because Constable Lewis thinks we were winding him up yesterday. We weren't, though, we were telling the truth."

Father Jacobs nodded in understanding. "This is about the smugglers, isn't it." He saw the surprise on the faces of the cousins. "Constable Lewis spent some time yesterday in the pub, telling anyone who would listen about you three and James trying to convince him that smugglers are using the island again."

Edward, Elizabeth, and Henri all studied the priest's face for any sign of what he thought about the previous day's events. He gave nothing away, however. For all they could tell, he could have been thinking anything, or nothing at all.

"Why don't we go and have a drink and talk about it," Father Jacobs suggested. He waited until all three teens had nodded their agreement, then he turned and led them away from the harbour.

The cousins expected to be led to The Stormy Teacup, which was close by. Instead, Father Jacobs took them to the church, where he guided them to the door that led to the vestry and then through to the rectory kitchen.

To the teens, the rectory's kitchen looked much like the one at the Bligh farm. It was pleasant and welcoming, with nothing to suggest it was either connected to a church or used by a man of the cloth.

"Please, sit down." Father Jacobs gestured to the chairs around the table. "I thought it might be better to talk here, rather than where someone might overhear and relay our conversation to people who might not take kindly to what we say. We also wouldn't want to cause any more trouble for James, should his aunt hear something she doesn't like and feel compelled to tell his father." He didn't elaborate on who might overhear, or who might not take kindly to what was said, but the cousins guessed he was talking about Constable Lewis and Sean Patricks.

"Okay." Father Jacobs took the seat at the head of the table once they all had drinks. "Since I've only heard second-hand, and probably garbled, accounts of yesterday, perhaps one of you should tell me what happened."

Edward only had to glance briefly from Elizabeth to Henri to see that he was the one expected to do the talking. It was often the case, so he was prepared for it, and after taking the time to get his thoughts in order, he began.

"Well, you three certainly had a busy day yesterday," Father Jacobs remarked once Edward had finished recounting the previous day's events. "I can almost understand why James' father grounded him. I had thought that what I heard yesterday afternoon was either garbled or exaggerated, but it seems that isn't the case.

"Did James really march into the police station and declare that Sean Patricks is a smuggler and call Lewis an idiot?"

"The first part, yes," Edward said. "The second part was me, but I was only repeating what we overheard."

"He didn't even want to listen to what we were trying to tell him," Henri said, aggrieved. "He never even considered that we might be telling the truth. He just decided we were playing a prank on him to make him look stupid, and that was it."

"That's hardly a surprise. Lewis is far from the most gifted of people, intellectually speaking, though he was, apparently, quite a decent bowler in his youth. In fact, I would go so far as to say he is frequently an idiot when it comes to things he has no previous experience with. I trust you won't repeat that," Father Jacobs said quickly.

Edward, Elizabeth, and Henri all laughed briefly, if awkwardly. Hearing a priest describe a constable as an idiot seemed wrong; to their minds, a priest was supposed to be polite and respectful towards everyone, but that was what made it amusing.

"You believe us about the smuggling, don't you, Father," Henri said. There was no response from Father Jacobs, though she waited for over a minute, and she finally prompted him, "Father Jacobs, you believe us, don't you?"

"What? Oh, yes," Father Jacobs said. "Sorry, I was just thinking about something. If this story had come from James and didn't involve the three of you, I think I would have a hard time believing it. After all, his reputation is against him in this kind of situation — he's well-known for his pranks and jokes."

"So, you believe James' story because of us?" Elizabeth asked, speaking for the first time since reaching the church.

Father Jacobs looked abashed. "The three of you certainly lend credence to the story. Your reputations are untainted as far as this island is concerned, but there are other reasons for me thinking the story is true.

"If James had set this up as a prank, the things you saw in the water would have still been there for Lewis to see, not just one box. A prank doesn't work very well without something to back it up. Not only that but James would never have continued the prank and tried to name Sean Patricks as the smuggler once it became clear it wasn't working. He knows when to give up on a joke."

Silence fell at the table for a short time as they finished their drinks. The silence continued for a bit beyond that as well, while Father Jacobs went and checked the church, in case anyone was wishing his assistance with anything.

He wasn't gone long, the church was empty, and once he returned the conversation resumed.

"What are you going to do?" Father Jacobs asked.

"Shouldn't we be asking you that?" Elizabeth asked.

"Perhaps," Father Jacobs said. "But the question is equally valid from either direction. You all took an enormous risk by exploring the path you discovered, one you really shouldn't have. You did, however, and now you need to decide what you are going to do about what you discovered.

"If you truly believe you stumbled on a smuggling ring, you have a duty to do something about it, especially since Lewis doesn't believe you."

"But what can we do?"

"I don't know," Father Jacobs admitted. "Ordinarily, I would say you should take this to the police, but that's clearly not an option. For my part, I will do what I can to help you, though I must be careful. The Bishop is unlikely to be happy if he discovers I'm investigating a possible smuggling ring instead of attending to my religious duties. Not that there's much for me to do here when it comes to that; Bligh Island only has a small congregation."

The debate over what they were going to do about the smuggling continued even after the cousins took their leave of Father Jacobs and left the rectory, without a resolution being reached.

They were as uncertain about what to do when they gave up on the discussion as they had been when the question was first asked.

23

The cousins were on their way back to the farm after an early lunch in The Stormy Teacup, having failed to think of anything else to do, when the peace they were enjoying was broken by the sound of a car engine.

The vehicle was no more than a speck on the horizon when they first looked. It quickly grew, though, and was soon recognisable as a bright red sports car, which they identified as a Porsche only when it was almost on top of them.

Eager to avoid being hit by the reckless driver, who either didn't know or didn't care that the island's wild inhabitants were prone to crossing the road at will, Edward, Elizabeth, and Henri moved away from the edge of the road. They kept parallel to it but put several feet between themselves and the tarmacked surface just in case the driver lost control and the Porsche left the road.

To the surprise of the cousins, not to mention their concern, the car slowed dramatically as it got closer.

For a second it seemed as though the Porsche was going to go into a skid, but then the driver got it under control and brought the vehicle to a stop level with them.

Nervous, and unsure of what was going on, the trio watched the car to see what was going to happen. So tightly wound were they by the situation that when the driver's door flew open, they all jumped, and Elizabeth gave a small scream of alarm.

Slowly, in contrast to how he had been driving, and how he had opened the door at his side, the driver got out.

When he straightened up and turned to the cousins, he revealed himself to be Sean Patricks, the man who had twice bumped into

Henri, and whom James had told Constable Lewis was a smuggler.

The moment they recognised him, the cousins felt their concerns increase, even Henri, though she did her best not to show it. She assumed a fierce expression and stared defiantly at Patricks.

"You're the Bligh kids, aren't you?" Patricks said, approaching them with a steady, unhurried step that reminded them of a killer in a horror movie.

None of them answered.

Even if his approach hadn't scared Edward, Elizabeth, and Henri, the fact that he knew who they were would have. They couldn't think how or why he knew their names, or why he had stopped to speak to them. The only possibilities that did come to their minds were not good.

"You are, aren't you? You're the ones who've been going around accusing me of being a smuggler, aren't you?"

None of the cousins could find the will to speak. They simply stood there, trying not to back away in fear. Even Henri, who was the bravest and boldest of them, had to work hard to resist the urge to retreat in the face of Patricks' approach.

"You don't need to answer, I know you are," Patricks said finally. "You should be careful about going to the police and accusing people of crimes without proof. That's the kind of thing that can get you in trouble, you and your little friend, James Allen. People don't like being accused of things, and the police don't like having their time wasted."

"We didn't waste police time," Henri said, finding her voice. "We reported what we found."

"Then how is it there was nothing there when you got the constable to your 'discovery'?" Patricks asked, a knowing look that was tinged with amusement on his face.

"Because you cleared it all up," Henri said. Anger overrode her fear and gave her the courage to talk back, despite him towering over her by almost a foot, being at least twice as heavy, and clearly possessing the strength to send her flying if he chose to hit her.

"That's just the kind of accusation you should be careful about," Patricks said. "There's so many bad things that can happen to people who throw around accusations like that, especially kids who go exploring dangerous places like cliffs far from anyone who could help them. Just imagine if one of you, or, God forbid, all of you, had fallen from that narrow path you found. Why, it could have been a long time before your bodies were found, if ever. I'll just bet you didn't tell anyone where you were going when you went exploring.

"If I were you, I'd think very carefully about interfering in business that has nothing to do with you. You all have bright futures ahead of you, I'm sure. If you can avoid poking your noses in where they don't belong, you might even get to enjoy them."

There was a blandness to Patricks' voice that made his thinly veiled threat all the more frightening to the cousins. None of them doubted that he would arrange an accident for them if they gave him cause to and would feel no guilt over doing so.

Abruptly, Patricks turned on his heel and returned to his car, where he slid behind the wheel. The engine was still running, and he sped away with a squeal from the tyres that left rubber marks that ran for a dozen feet along the road.

It was several long moments before the cousins reacted to what had happened. Even Henri, who had more guts than both her cousins combined, needed some time to recover from the shock of having her life threatened. It was not something she had ever thought would happen to her.

None of them could believe how much things had changed. What had started as a boring holiday, far from their friends and anything fun, was quickly turning into something else, something both more exciting and more dangerous.

"We need to tell Constable Lewis what just happened," Elizabeth said, trembling like a leaf. She had never felt as scared as she had during the last few minutes, and she hoped she never would again. She clutched at her brother for support and comfort and wished fervently that they had never gone looking for the old smuggler's cave. It had caused them nothing but trouble.

"What good's that going to do?" Henri wanted to know, recovering her calm quicker than her cousins.

"He threatened us," Elizabeth said, as though the younger girl had not realised what had happened.

"I know he did. But telling Constable Lewis won't make any difference."

"Why do you say that?" Edward asked. He agreed with her but wondered if her reasons were the same as his own.

"Because he's an idiot," Henri said without hesitation. "He didn't believe us yesterday, so why would he believe us now. It would be our word against Patricks', and Lewis has already decided we're liars."

Edward nodded. "You're right. Even if Lewis believed us and spoke to Patricks, it wouldn't do any good. Patricks would either say we made the whole thing up or it was a misunderstanding, and he was simply advising us not to accuse him of breaking the law without proof and warning us that we should be careful about exploring strange places because it could be dangerous. I'm sure it would sound very reasonable to Lewis, especially since he's not very bright and he didn't hear the way Patricks was speaking. We've got no witnesses who can back us up, so it's our word against his."

"What do we do then, if we can't go to the police?" Elizabeth wanted to know. "Tell Brenda and Lloyd? They seemed to believe us yesterday, they might believe us about this as well."

"We need to tell James, I know that much, but I'm not sure about telling Brenda and Lloyd. If they believe us, they might overreact and do something stupid."

"Like what?" Elizabeth couldn't imagine what could be more stupid than them exploring a tunnel and cliff path when they didn't know where it led or if it was safe.

"I don't know," Edward admitted. "All I am sure of right now, other than that we need to tell James what just happened, so he knows to be careful, is that we need to get back to the farm before Patricks drives back this way. And we should keep a careful eye out, so we can avoid him in the future." With that said, he started walking.

He was tempted to cut across country and take the most direct route to the farm in case Patricks drove back that way more quickly than they anticipated. He decided against doing so, however, figuring they would make quicker time if they stuck close to the road.

"YOU'RE NOT REALLY GOING to go along with James' plan, are you?" Elizabeth asked of her brother. They were walking around the farm with Henri, supposedly to help their food go down, but really because they didn't want to be overheard by Brenda or Lloyd.

Edward didn't answer straight away, instead, he wandered idly in the direction of the sheep who were grazing in the field they had entered. He gave himself until he reached the nearest of the woolly animals, which showed no concern at his presence, to think about the question. It didn't help.

"I don't know," he admitted unhappily, reaching out to feel the sheep's fleece. He had been wondering what wool felt like, before it became wool, since he saw the sheep that Brenda and Lloyd kept. He didn't like being indecisive, but he could think of good reasons both for and against going along with the plan James had come up with, seemingly on the spur of the moment.

When they had called James to warn him, they had worried that his father would answer and refuse to let them speak to him. Thankfully, James' father had been at work, so they hadn't had to worry about him intercepting the call or overhearing them as they discussed their encounter with Sean Patricks that afternoon.

They were all sure that if James' father had heard them, there would be no possibility of James getting out of the house again before the end of the holidays, and certainly no possibility of them doing anything about the smugglers.

"But James said he's going, whether we go with him or not. If he's right, it could be dangerous for him on his own."

"If James is right," Elizabeth said, "it will be dangerous, no matter how many of us go."

"Well, I don't care about the danger," Henri declared, copying Edward and running her fingers through the fleece of the placid sheep next to her. She was surprised and disappointed by how dirty the sheep was up close; it was nowhere near as white as it had looked from a distance. "I've already decided, I'm going with James in the morning. I want to see if we can find some evidence to prove we're not liars." It didn't matter to her that she was never likely to see Constable Lewis again once the holidays were over; he thought they were liars and she wanted to prove him wrong.

Elizabeth looked at her cousin in disbelief. "You can't be serious. It's one thing for Edward to think about going, at least he'd have a chance of defending himself if James is right, but how can you even think about going? James' idea is stupid and dangerous. What if you encounter Mr Patricks?"

"It's not stupid," Henri defended her friend. "Besides, if Constable Lewis isn't going to believe us, what can we do but try and find evidence to prove we're right."

"I'm going as well," Edward said suddenly, making up his mind and announcing his decision to try and head off the argument that was brewing between his sister and his cousin. "You can stay here tomorrow, if you like, Elizabeth, but I think it's best if I go. I can keep them out of trouble." He looked sideways at Henri and added, "Hopefully."

24

Edward didn't want to startle Elizabeth and Henri awake by turning on the big light, so he felt his way through the darkness of the room, using the wall and the furniture as guides, until he reached the bedside table on the near side of the bed.

Once there he searched the top of it with his fingertips for the lamp. The lamp was old, and its bulb weak, but it provided enough light for him to see his sister and his cousin.

Henri's eyes fluttered open the moment the lamp went on and she rolled towards the light, entangling herself further in the duvet.

In contrast, Elizabeth remained asleep and unmoving, oblivious to the sudden light. She didn't stir until Edward gently shook her shoulder.

"Is it morning already?" Elizabeth asked in a quiet and sleep-filled voice when she made out the figure of her brother standing over her through half-closed eyes.

"Yes," Edward answered in a voice that was barely above a whisper. "James will be here soon if he hasn't overslept or been caught by his dad, so you'd better get up." He glanced over at Henri and saw that she needed no help to wake up, she had already untangled herself from the duvet and thrown back her side of it so she could get out of bed.

Since the girls were awake, if not yet with it, Edward left them to sort themselves out and made for the bathroom. He had a quick wash and then returned to his bedroom to get dressed.

In barely five minutes he was downstairs, chewing on a thick slice of bread and jam to quiet his stomach, and waiting for his sister and his cousin.

Elizabeth and Henri joined Edward soon enough, dressed alike in jeans, jumpers, and jackets to keep themselves warm, and wearing footwear suitable for walking and exploring. They helped themselves to some of the bread and jam that Edward had prepared and chewed on it slowly while they waited, shivering a little in the coolness of the pre-dawn air and trying not to yawn.

Their breakfast, such as it was, was gone, and they were just beginning to think he wasn't going to show up before Brenda and Lloyd got up to start their day on the farm when a barely audible knock at the back door announced the arrival of James.

"Are we all set?" he asked in a quiet voice the moment the door was opened to admit him. He didn't enter, instead, he remained on the doorstep, eager to get going.

Edward nodded and let Elizabeth and Henri out of the house first before closing the door behind him as quietly as he could. He glanced briefly through the window on his way past and saw that the note he had left for Brenda and Lloyd, in which he told them they had gone exploring with James, had fallen over. It was still visible, though, and would be found easily when they came down for breakfast.

He figured Brenda would worry despite the note, even if Lloyd didn't, but at least the note would make it less likely that she would search for them out of concern over their absence.

The journey to the tunnel passed in silence, with James leading the way across the countryside. None of them was awake enough for idle talk, and even if they had been, they needed what concentration they had to make sure they didn't trip or get a foot stuck in a rabbit hole.

The light was improving as dawn neared, but they still couldn't see further than twenty feet in any direction by the time they reached the entrance to the tunnel.

"I'm going first," Edward said in a voice that brooked no argument. "Elizabeth, you and Henri come next, James, you bring up the rear." His instructions given, he took a torch from the bag James had brought, turned it on, and climbed into the hole.

The tunnel was no darker than it had been the last time he went through it, yet Edward couldn't help feeling more on edge this time. He wasn't sure if it was the fact that it was so early in the morning and it was still mostly dark beyond the tunnel or the knowledge that they might encounter someone at their destination that made him feel that way. Whatever it was, his eyes darted everywhere, searching every shadow for a danger that never appeared, and checking over his shoulder to be sure the others were alright.

Henri, who was next in line, showed no fear, only tiredness, while Elizabeth was scared, but doing her best not to show it, though Edward, who knew his sister so well, could see it in her eyes. James could have been thinking anything or nothing at all for all that Edward could see of him at the back of the line; he was only just about to tell that James was with them.

Soon enough the tunnel ended, and the four teens were again out in the fresh air. They were fortunate that the path was on the South-Eastern side of the island, where it gained the maximum amount of light at that time of the morning. Even so, Edward found it advisable to light his way with the torch.

Slowly, and with the greatest of care, he made his way down the path, ever conscious that he could lose his footing at any moment if he didn't pay enough attention.

"I was right, the tide is out," James said when they reached the end of the path and saw the narrow strip of rocky ground that had been exposed by the retreating tide.

"You mean you weren't sure it would be?" Elizabeth asked, her disbelief and annoyance overriding, temporarily, her fear of where they were and what they were doing. "You said you know the tides."

"I do. I just couldn't be certain the tide would clear this area. I've not been here at low tide before, so I had to guess. I was sure I wouldn't be far off, though. I'd guess we've got a couple of hours, maybe three, before the tide starts turning and the water gets too deep for us to get

back to the path. If we're going to do this, we'd better get on with it."
He was eager to find the evidence to prove that he had been right about
Patricks being a smuggler and that for once he hadn't been lying or
playing a prank.

Edward led the way across the strip of exposed ground, wondering
as he moved carefully over the wet rock how far it went. He soon found
the answer when he followed the beach — it was the only word he
could think of to describe it — around the curve of the cliff.

The cliff had been eroded by the sea at that point and the beach
disappeared into the shadow of the island's bulk for about half the
length of a football field before ending abruptly.

If it hadn't been for the torch he held, Edward wouldn't have seen
the cave until he was right on top of it. Even with the light from the
torch to aid him, he had to get within twenty-five feet of the cave before
he was sure he had found what they were looking for, and he wasn't just
seeing a darker patch of the cliff.

He suspected that that was how Solomon Kierney had got away
with his smuggling for so long. The entrance to the cave was a black
hole about eight feet high by ten feet wide and it blended into the dark
rock of the cliff, making it almost impossible to see unless you were
right on top of it.

There was just enough space for a small boat to enter the cave if
it was handled carefully, though it wasn't possible at that time for half
a dozen feet of rocky beach separated the cave from the waters that
surrounded Bligh Island.

"THIS IS THE PLACE," Edward said, shining his torch around the
opening he had discovered.

"I told you it was here," James said excitedly, moving past Elizabeth
and Henri so he could approach the cave. He was eager to get on with

exploring.

"Keep it down." As always, Elizabeth was the cautious one in the group, the one who realised what a bad idea it was for them to make too much noise. "We don't want anyone to know we're here," she said, pitching her voice at a level she hoped wouldn't carry.

With a marked degree of reluctance, Edward, Henri, and James all lowered their voices.

Despite the reduced volume, they couldn't entirely conceal their pleasure at finding the cave they were looking for, the cave that others had looked for, without success, for the past two hundred years.

After several long moments, they got themselves under control and got on with what they were there to do. As a group, and with no thought for the sensibly safe single file line they had maintained previously, they hurried forward to examine the cave.

Edward and Elizabeth both paused for the briefest of moments on the threshold, while Henri and James entered the cave without hesitation, their path illuminated by the torch in James' hand.

"Well, I guess that explains how they get their cargos in here," Edward said quietly as he joined Henri and James. The light from his and James' torches shone on the surface of a dark, limpid pool that started just a few feet inside the cave and quickly spread out to fill it, becoming almost twenty feet wide as the cave broadened and continuing to the back, thirty feet away. "When the tide's in, this must connect to the sea, and be deep enough for a boat to enter."

James turned his light away from the pool. "I'd say you're right." He illuminated a wet line that ran around the edge of the cave and marked the high tide point for the pool. "Looks like the water gets about three feet deep through the entrance. They'd only be able to use a boat with a shallow draft, but it'd definitely be possible to get a boat in here. Two, if they were careful."

"So, they can get boats in," Henri said. "What do they do with the cargo when they've unloaded it?" She searched the darkness with her eyes but could see no sign of either a cargo or a place where it could be stashed. Nor could she see any way out of the cave other than how they had entered.

Since the cave existed, proving that at least part of the story of the smuggler was true, she assumed the rest of the story was true as well, which meant there should be a tunnel leading out of the cave and up through the cliff to what remained of Solomon Kierney's house.

"I think we go this way," James said after a moment. His eyesight was no sharper than that of his fellow teens, but he did have the advantage of being able to direct the light from the torch he held, which meant he could see things a little better.

A narrow ledge, no more than a foot and a half wide, ran around the pool, hugging the side of the cave, and he led the way along it to the patch of deeper black that he had spotted in the darkness.

The quartet stopped in the entrance to the tunnel and held a hurried discussion about what they were going to do.

Elizabeth was all for going back. As far as she was concerned, they had done enough to prove they were telling the truth, though she reluctantly admitted that Constable Lewis still might not believe them.

Edward wanted his sister and Henri to stay in the cave while he and James continued exploring, so they could go for help if there was any trouble.

James didn't care what the others did. He intended searching for proof that Constable Lewis couldn't ignore, no matter how long it took him to find it.

It fell to Henri to make the final decision, not that any of them asked her to. Annoyed that they were standing around talking, instead of doing something, when they only had a limited amount of time available to them, she snatched the torch from Edward's hand and strode quickly down the tunnel they had discovered.

The light from the torch revealing rough walls, with many stones sharp enough to draw blood, an uneven floor, which seemed eager to trip the unwary, and a roof that would have been a danger to her skull if she had been as tall as the average man.

Edward was caught by surprise by Henri's initiative and had no chance to stop her. By the time he realised what she had done he was left with no choice but to follow her, along with Elizabeth and James, who both realised they couldn't let Henri go off on her own.

"Should we be using the torches," Elizabeth asked nervously before they had gone even a dozen feet into the tunnel. "If Mr Patricks or any of his smuggling gang are down here, they'll see the light from our torches long before we'll see them."

Edward knew his sister was right, but there was a more important consideration than the possibility of them being discovered. "If we turn the torches off, we won't be able to see where we're going." He kept his voice quiet, almost a whisper, but it still seemed to echo up and down the tunnel with a volume greater than that used by him. "Who knows what sort of trouble we'd get into then. We could walk into a wall or fall down a hole."

When she heard Edward mention the possibility of holes in the floor, something she hadn't considered, Henri slowed her pace and moved with greater caution.

No holes in the ground, dropping away towards the centre of the earth, showed themselves in the light from her torch. She did, however, find an opening in the wall of the tunnel.

With more caution than she was normally inclined to show, Henri paused at the side of the opening. She peered around the edge, illuminating the darkness with her torch to check for dangers, whether human or natural, and discovered what she had found was a cave, rather than another tunnel.

It held no dangers that she could see, only boxes like those they had seen in the surf the other day.

Since there appeared to be nothing to worry about, Henri entered the cave so she could investigate the boxes.

James moved forward as eagerly as Henri, keen to check out the contents of the cave. Edward also entered the cave without hesitation, curiosity drawing him to the boxes, just as it did the other two. Elizabeth, however, hung back, her curiosity overwhelmed by her concern that Sean Patricks, or one of his accomplices, might sneak up on them.

She remained by the cave's entrance, where she could keep an eye and ear out for approaching danger, while the others searched the cave's contents.

"I think this is the stuff we saw the other day," Edward said as he walked around the boxes haphazardly piled to one side of the cave and lifted the flaps on those that had been torn open to see what they contained. "I thought Patricks said he got rid of it all."

"He said he recovered it all, and it would have to be replaced," Henri said, recalling the one-sided conversation they had overheard. "He must have dumped it in here out of the way. I can't see any of the undamaged stuff they must have brought in at the same time. They can't have got rid of it already, can they?"

Edward shrugged. "Maybe, or maybe they've got it somewhere else. What've you got over there?" He moved away from the pile he was examining to cross the cave to where Henri and James were checking out a collection of wooden crates at the back.

The crates bore no markings to indicate their age, but their appearance suggested years of neglect. They were rotted and falling apart and looked as though the slightest touch would be enough to make them crumble into pieces.

"A bunch of old stuff," James said. "Really old. It must have been here since Kierney got caught. It's hard to tell what some of it is, but this," he took a bottle from one of the crates and held it up, "must be rum. That's what Kierney used to smuggle a lot of according to Father J." There was a label on the bottle, but it was no longer possible to make out anything of what had been on it.

"I think this might have been tobacco." Henri lifted a handful of the contents from another crate and let it trickle through her fingers. Whatever it had been once, it was now little more than dust, so fine that it was barely visible as it drifted down.

James' curiosity led him to work the cork free from the bottle he held so he could sniff the contents. The smell was strong enough to make his nose wrinkle and his eyes water. It was nothing like his father's rum, which he had smelled when his father had a drink, and he was sure it would be a bad idea to have so much as a sip.

He suspected the alcohol would have been dangerous to drink when it was freshly made, let alone after spending the best part of two hundred years neglected in a cave.

Blinking to clear his eyes, he tried to recork the bottle, without success. After several tries, he gave up and returned the bottle to the crate, still open. He hoped it wouldn't be noticed. He didn't think it would, the crate and its contents had been there for so long, he doubted whether Sean Patricks or his fellow smugglers paid it any heed.

When they found nothing else of interest in the cave, they left to continue their exploration, this time with James in the lead.

"WHAT'S THAT?" ELIZABETH asked in a hoarse, scared voice a few moments after they left a second cave, whose contents, unlike those of the first cave, were intact and obviously new.

More than three dozen boxes of various sizes had filled the cave, and it was clear that Sean Patricks' gang of smugglers were organised for the boxes were separated into neat piles, each of which contained something different. One pile was mobile phones and tablet devices, another DVDs, Blu-Rays, and CDs, a third contained box after box of cigarettes and tobacco, the most popular brands, while the last pile was made up of alcohol.

"I didn't hear anything," James said from the front of the group, where he was again leading them.

"I did," Edward said, straining to listen.

"*...things to do this afternoon, and I want to make sure everything's sorted and ready for tonight. We've got a lot to do.*"

"*We should have got a couple of the guys over to help then, it would've sped things up.*"

The first voice was hard to identify because the owner was speaking quietly, and his words were distorted by the echoing effect of the tunnel, but James was sure it belonged to Sean Patricks, and he was clearly annoyed.

"*How many times do I have to tell you? If we bring any of the guys over during the day they might get seen, and then the locals will start wondering what's going on. We can get the work done between us, as long as you don't start slacking, and the guys can handle the loading tonight, while we relax and supervise.*"

"Quick, back the way we came," Edward said in a sharp whisper as he made an about-face and set off down the tunnel away from the voices, which were getting closer.

Edward was tempted to tell Henri and James to turn off the torches as he led the way at speed away from the danger. He realised it wouldn't be a good idea, though; without the light, it was likely that one of them, if not all, would trip on the uneven floor of the tunnel, and that would leave them vulnerable to capture by the smugglers.

Rapid footsteps from right behind him, and the wavering of the torchlight that guided him, told Edward that the others were following him. He was relieved. He had no idea what would happen to them if they were caught, but he didn't imagine it would be anything good. He was sure the smugglers would want to keep them from going to the police and might not be too fussy about how they did so.

From farther back in the tunnel came the footsteps and the voices of the smugglers, and Edward couldn't help thinking that it hadn't been such a good idea for them to go looking for proof that smuggling was taking place.

It was one thing to imagine a risk from the comfort of safety, and another to face that risk. Even the most benign possibility that sprang to his mind seemed much worse in the semi-darkness of the tunnel and made his heart race.

When he stumbled and nearly fell, he forced his mind away from what might be, and away from what they should or shouldn't have done, and back on the here and now. The only thing that mattered at that moment was getting out of there safely.

No sooner had he recovered his balance, thankfully without suffering an injury, than a startled cry came from behind him. The torchlight danced crazily around the tunnel as his ears were filled with the sound of falling bodies and a series of moans and groans.

A heartbeat later one of the torches went out, halving the amount of light and allowing the darkness to creep closer.

Fearing the worst, Edward spun around. In the light from the remaining torch, he saw Elizabeth at the bottom of a pile of bodies, with James and Henri on top of her.

"What happened?" he asked in an urgent whisper once he had helped them untangle their limbs and get to their feet.

"I tripped," Elizabeth admitted, embarrassed. "They must have tripped over me." She had injured herself again, she was sure, but just then any injuries were of little concern to her. "It doesn't matter, we have to get out of here." She couldn't tell if the smugglers had heard her fall, she hoped not, but she could still hear them coming.

To emphasise the urgency she felt, she bent to pick up the still working torch and then pushed past her brother so she could hurry along the tunnel.

She was moving so quickly she was surprised she didn't trip over again. Despite that concern, she didn't slow. Tripping was less of a worry for her than being caught.

The end of the tunnel came so abruptly that Elizabeth almost strode straight into the pool. She managed to stop in time, to her relief, and turned to follow the path around to the cave's entrance. It was easy to see, thanks to the pale light of the early morning sun that shone through the opening, and the sight of it spurred her on.

She was so pleased to be back out in the fresh air that the turning of the tide, which swamped her trainers and soaked her socks and feet, didn't bother her. She had never enjoyed having wet feet, and wet socks were one of the worst things ever in her opinion. Just then, however, she didn't care. Wet socks and feet were a small price to pay to be away from the smugglers, whom she had been sure were going to grab her at any moment.

Now she was out of the cave and the darkness her fears faded. The danger seemed so much farther away in daylight when she could see everything around her easily.

"We need to hurry," James said urgently from behind Elizabeth. "We must have been in there longer than I thought."

He was not concerned with Sean Patricks and his smuggler friend, though that danger was not entirely past. It was the incoming tide that worried him, which he realised was a bigger threat to them than the smugglers.

If they were caught by Patricks, there was a chance they could beg for mercy, or somehow overpower him and his friend. The tide had no mercy, however. No amount of persuasion would convince it to let them go once it had them in its grasp, and there was no hope of them overpowering it.

As quickly as they could with their clothes and their trainers soaked and heavy, they made their way along the stony beach to the path that led up to the top of the cliff.

25

"Oh no!" Elizabeth cried in distress when they finally reached the top of the cliff.

"What?" Edward let go of Henri, whom he had been helping from the tunnel below the gorse bush, and spun around to check on his sister.

From the tone of Elizabeth's voice, he expected to find them surrounded by Sean Patricks and his gang of smugglers, all of them armed with menacing looks and deadly weapons. There was no one, though, they were alone on the clifftop.

"I've lost my phone," Elizabeth said, making it sound as though she had lost a limb.

For several long moments, Edward stared at his sister in disbelief. Her cry had set his heart to racing, and it took a short time to settle down again.

"I thought something serious had happened," he said finally.

"It has," Elizabeth said. "I've lost my phone. It's got everything on it, practically my whole life, including the pictures I took of everything down there. Without my phone, we've got no proof. That means we risked our lives for nothing. It was all a waste of time."

James shook his head. He had emerged from the tunnel in time to hear Elizabeth's comment. "Not for nothing," he said. "We know when the rest of the gang's coming to take away what's in the cave, and they'll probably be bringing some more stuff in. That's something."

"What good is that? Constable Lewis is never going to believe us without proof." Elizabeth made to re-enter the tunnel but was stopped by Edward, who caught her around the waist as she tried to go past him. "We have to go back and find my phone," she said, her voice urgent, though whether that urgency was because she wanted proof for

Constable Lewis or because she couldn't bear the thought of losing all her contacts and photos was hard to tell.

"Do you know where you lost it?" Edward asked, surprised, not only by the fact that she was prepared to go back for her phone when she knew the smugglers were around but also by the strength with which Elizabeth fought against his grip. She couldn't get free, he was strong enough to keep hold of her, but it wasn't for lack of trying.

Elizabeth stopped her struggling for a moment so she could fix her brother with a withering look. "If I knew when and where I lost it, don't you think I'd have stopped to pick it up? The last time I'm sure I had it is in the second cave. I know I had it then because I took pictures of the boxes and what was in them."

"So, you could have lost it anywhere between here and there. If that's the case, there's going to be just about no chance of finding it. If you dropped it on the path, it's almost certainly gone over the edge, and if you dropped it on the beach, it'll be under the sea by now. Either way, you won't find it, and it'd be useless if you could."

"I might have dropped it in the tunnel when I tripped over," Elizabeth said. "In fact, I'm sure I must have dropped it then. I don't remember having it when I got up. If I did drop it there, it's probably still going to be working when we get it back, so we can show Constable Lewis the pictures I took, then he'll have to believe us when we tell him the smugglers are coming back tonight." She renewed her efforts to free herself from her brother, only to stop again when James spoke.

"You won't have any more luck getting your phone back if you dropped it in the tunnel than if you dropped it in the sea," he said. "You can't get back to the tunnel now, the tide's come in too far. If you try and go back, you'll almost certainly get swept off your feet and slammed against the cliff. Most likely you'd be killed." The uncertainty on Elizabeth's face suggested she didn't know whether to believe him or not, so he went on, "Even if you could get back round to the cave without being swept away, we know Patricks is down in the tunnels.

Chances are either he or his friend would find you before you could find your phone, assuming they haven't found it themselves."

Reluctantly, and only after almost a minute, did Elizabeth accept what James had said. She wasn't happy about it, but she knew she had to accept that there was nothing she could do about the situation.

THE FRONT DOOR OF THE farmhouse flew open as the quartet of teens, tired from lost sleep and their early morning exertions, made their way across the yard.

In the doorway stood Brenda, a furious look on her face, though she said nothing until all the teens were inside and she had closed the door behind them.

"Do you have any idea how worried we've been?" she demanded. "How could you sneak out like thieves in the night, with nothing but a note to tell us where you'd gone?" Her voice filled the house, not just the passage, as she shepherded the teens towards the kitchen. "Anything could have happened to you, anything, did you consider that?"

"We were careful," Edward said defensively. "We waited until the sun was up before we went down the path, and we timed our arrival so the tide was out. We had rope and a first-aid kit with us as well just in case anything happened."

"We knew what we were doing," James spoke up.

"How on earth can you say you knew what you were doing?" Brenda demanded, rounding on James. "You took a narrow and dangerous cliff path, with dawn still breaking, so you could look for a cave you believe is used by smugglers. If that isn't the dumbest thing you've ever done, James Allen, then I'm a monkey's auntie."

That comment would have brought a smile to James' lips if he wasn't being shouted at.

"Not only did you put yourself at risk, which is bad enough, you risked Elizabeth and Henri as well by persuading them to go along with you. Any of you could have fallen off the path, no matter how careful you were, or even all of you, and if we hadn't found your note we wouldn't have known where to look for you. As it is, I had to talk Lloyd out of going off on his own to find you. Though given how long it's taken Lewis to get here, he might as well have done."

Lloyd glowered at the teens from the kitchen table but said nothing.

"What if you had been right about the smugglers? What if you had run into them while you were down there? They could have done anything to you. Did you think of that? I doubt they would have wanted to take a chance on you lot giving them away." Brenda paused for a moment to take some deep breaths to try to get herself under control, which she was only partially successful in doing. "Can you imagine the kind of thoughts that have been going through our minds?"

"We wouldn't have had to do this if Lewis had believed us," James said, almost defiantly.

"So, it's Lewis' fault that you decided to sneak out before dawn, put your life, and the lives of your friends, at risk, and worry the people who care about you all so much you could have given them heart attacks." Brenda's anger flared again, making her face go red. "What about your father and your aunt? Do they know where you went, or what you've been doing? I'll bet you didn't even leave them a note."

The embarrassed look on James' face answered that question without him needing to say anything.

"Lewis thinks we're lying about the smugglers." Was all James could think of to say.

"And how was going back down there supposed to have convinced him you were telling the truth?"

"We were after proof," Edward answered for James.

"And we found it," James said, a satisfied look on his face. "We found the cave, and the stuff Sean Patricks has been smuggling, and we know when his gang's coming back. They're coming tonight to pick up what's in the cave, and probably to drop off some more stuff."

"And where is this proof?" Lloyd asked.

"We lost it," Elizabeth admitted. She was reluctant to speak, given how angry Brenda was; the stern look on Lloyd's face didn't encourage her, but she felt she had to since it was the loss of her phone that made what they had done a waste of time. "I took a bunch of pictures of everything we saw down there, but I dropped my phone on the way back out."

"So, you've got no proof," Lloyd said. "You risked your lives for nothing."

Things got no better for the teens when Constable Lewis arrived twenty minutes later. He was not as angry as Brenda, but he was still far from pleased with what they had done, a description of which he listened to with barely concealed impatience.

"I should charge you all with being a nuisance and wasting police time," Lewis said when Edward and James had finished their account of what they had been up to. "This may not be a busy island when it comes to crime, but that doesn't mean I don't have things to do, things I have to interrupt to deal with this kind of stupid behaviour. How do you think people would feel if they learned that I couldn't deal with their problem because a bunch of kids with no sense decided to put their lives at risk because they believe smugglers are using this island like it's the eighteen-hundreds all over again?

"If I thought it'd do any good, I'd charge you. It'd just be an even bigger waste of my time, though. Even if you did get prosecuted, the worst you'd get is a slap on the wrist, and I doubt you three, being rich and related to the baron," he waved a hand at Edward, Elizabeth, and Henri, "would even get that much. Since there's no point in me punishing you, I'll leave it to your father, James. I'm sure he'll come up with something far worse than I could, and to you two, Brenda, Lloyd, to punish them.

"If any of you cause me any more trouble, though, I will charge you, and I'll see to it you get prosecuted, rich family and titled relations or not. Now, James, you come with me. Let's see what your father has to say about this morning's fun."

There was a gleam in Constable Lewis' eye that spoke eloquently of his pleasure at the thought of the punishment he was sure James was going to receive from his father.

James, though he tried not to show it, looked worried.

"WHAT ARE WE GOING TO do?" Henri asked as Edward slipped into the bedroom to join her and Elizabeth.

The punishment the teens had received at the hands of Brenda and Lloyd was not as severe as it could have been. It was certainly not as severe as they were all sure Constable Lewis would have liked it to be. It was harsh enough, in the opinion of the cousins, for whom serious trouble was rare, and harsh punishments even rarer.

They had been grounded for the rest of the holiday and were to help with all chores around the farm, no matter how menial or disgusting they might seem.

"What can we do?" Elizabeth asked a question of her own. Tucking her legs under her, she made space on the bed for her brother to sit down. "We've been grounded. Even if we hadn't been, there's nothing we can do, we're just kids." It wasn't an admission she liked to make, she generally thought of herself as being fairly adult, despite her age, but it wasn't something she could entirely deny. "It'd be different if I hadn't lost my phone, or if Constable Lewis believed us. Right now, though, we don't even have Brenda or Lloyd on our side."

"They believe us," Henri said.

"Do they?" Elizabeth wasn't so sure. "Even if they do, what can they do? The only person who can do anything is Constable Lewis, and since he doesn't believe us, he won't. I think it's time we just forget about it." Doing so would mean she would have to forget about her phone as well, a prospect she didn't like, but it was better than the alternative to her mind. "If we try and do anything else, we're just going to get ourselves into even more trouble, maybe even get ourselves hurt. Really hurt, I mean, not just cuts and scrapes, but hospital hurt."

"We have to do something," Edward said. "They're breaking the law. You've heard all about the results of modern smuggling." He knew his sister had heard the same news reports he had and watched the same documentaries in social science class. "What gets funded by the money the smugglers make, and how many people get hurt."

Elizabeth nodded unhappily. "I know all that, but there's nothing we can do. It's a job for the police, that's what they're paid to do, to stop people like Sean Patricks."

"Except Constable Lewis doesn't believe us and isn't going to do anything," Henri said.

"And there's nothing we can do about that." Elizabeth rounded on her cousin. She did her best to keep her voice low, to avoid being overheard by Brenda and Lloyd, who were downstairs. "Unless you think we should take the law into our own hands. Which would be completely ridiculous," she said quickly when she saw that Henri was about to say something. "We're kids, they're adults. There's no way we'd stand a chance of stopping them. It'd be stupid of us to even try."

Silence fell between the three teens for a while as their thoughts meandered from one idea to the next, without settling on anything. All of them were thinking about the situation they had got themselves into, though their minds headed in different directions.

Elizabeth was wishing they could go back to the start of their holiday, which wasn't so long ago, and avoid getting mixed up in anything to do with smugglers.

Edward was trying to think of a way to convince Constable Lewis that they were telling the truth about the smugglers, even though they lacked proof.

Henri meanwhile was trying to work out how a group of teens, none of whom were skilled at fighting, or even all that large, could hope to stop a gang of smugglers without help from at least one adult. It didn't seem possible to her, though her optimistic nature made her certain there must be a way.

It was Edward who finally broke the silence.

"What about Father Jacobs?" he said, surprising the other two with the sudden question. "He said he was going to help us if he could."

"What can he do?" Elizabeth asked. "He's only a priest."

"I know he's only a priest, but he said he'd help us if he can," Edward said. "Maybe he'll be able to think of something we can't. If we tell him what's happened and he says he can't help us, we haven't lost anything, have we?"

Elizabeth considered her brother's suggestion, looking at it from all the angles, and was forced to admit that he was right. "How do we get hold of him, though?" she asked. "We can't go down to the church because we've been grounded." She wasn't sure what Brenda and Lloyd would do if they broke their grounding and went to the church, she wasn't sure there was much they could do since they weren't their parents, but neither was she keen on finding out. "And we don't know his number or the church's. We can't ask Brenda for the number either. She'll know we're up to something the moment we do."

"James," Edward said in answer. "James can give us Father Jacobs' number, or he can speak to him himself."

"And how do we contact James? Our phones are next to useless out here. It's hard enough to keep a signal long enough to send a message, let alone trying to make a call." Elizabeth had tried to make several calls during the first week of their holiday on the island, without much success. Even in Blighton, the signal was too weak to be reliable. "We can't use the phone downstairs, either, since we're not supposed to have anything to do with James now."

In addition to not being allowed to leave the farm and having to help with the chores that were required to keep the farm going, Brenda and Lloyd had declared that Edward, Elizabeth, and Henri were not allowed to have anything more to do with James. Since he was the reason they had gone exploring and put themselves at risk to find the smuggler's cave, Brenda and Lloyd had decided that the teens were less likely to get into any more trouble if they stayed away from James for the rest of the holidays.

Edward smiled and tapped Elizabeth's laptop. "Facebook, of course," he said, as though the answer should have been obvious. He pulled the laptop closer and opened the Facebook page on his sister's internet browser. He was pleased to see that James was online, meaning he hadn't been banned from social media by his dad, and they wouldn't have to wait for a reply.

"*What happened when you got home?*" Edward typed without preamble.

"*Lewis told dad I snuck out, he hadn't even realised I wasn't home, and where I went. He grounded me, again! Big deal. You?*" James replied though it took a while for his reply to come through.

"*Grounded,*" Edward typed. "*We've got to stay on the farm and do chores, and we're not supposed to have anything to do with you anymore.*" He reassured James that despite the injunction they had been given, neither he, Elizabeth, nor Henri would be abandoning their friendship with him.

"*Wow!*" James was surprised by the punishment. The grounding and the chores he had expected, but he had never thought Brenda and Lloyd would go so far as to forbid contact with him. That seemed like an overreaction to him.

"*Could have been worse,*" Edward typed. "*If they didn't need the money they're being paid to look after us, they'd probably be thinking of* sending us home."

"Will they change their mind?"

Edward responded with an emoticon shrug. "Maybe. There's something more important we need to worry about, though. What can we do about Patricks? Can you get hold of Father Jacobs?"

"Probs. Why?"

"He said he'd help us. Maybe he can think of a way to stop Patricks."

"I'll call him, see what he says. BRB."

Edward, Elizabeth, and Henri were left to wait for several minutes for James to return, during which time they listened nervously for any indication that Brenda might be coming to check on them.

When James finally returned to his computer, he had bad news.

"Father J's not in. Answer message says he's gone to the mainland and won't be back till later. No answer on his mobile," James typed. "What do we do?"

"No idea," Edward admitted. "Hoped you'd have one."

James' response was immediate, but far from helpful. "Need proof. Can't let Patricks get away with this. Can't let Lewis believe I'm a liar either."

"Agreed. How do we get proof, though?"

"Go back."

"You mad?" Edward typed back quickly, while Elizabeth and Henri followed the conversation on the screen over his shoulder.

"Maybe. Hope not. Have to go back, tho, Lewis won't stop Patricks without proof. Need to get it."

"How? All grounded. Plus, tide's in."

It was almost a minute before James responded. "Tide out again from five. Go then."

"How? Grounded! Can't get out."

"Have to." James couldn't have said why he was so determined to stop Sean Patricks, other than that he wanted to prove Lewis wrong, but he felt a need to do so, despite the potential risks, and the knowledge that Sean Patricks had already threatened his friends. *"Go alone if have to."*

Edward couldn't believe James would be foolish enough to even consider going to the cave on his own to get proof the smugglers existed. *"Can't, it's too dangerous."*

"If you won't come with me, have to."

"You alone or all of us, how do we stop them? They're adults, we're kids." He was the biggest of them, but Edward wasn't stupid enough to think he could match a man in any kind of a fight, not even if he were inclined towards fighting, which he wasn't.

"Not stop," James typed quickly. *"Get proof. If we're lucky we can get in and out while Patricks and his gang aren't there. We can get photos to convince Lewis, then he can stop them."* He wasn't entirely convinced of that, but he figured that if they gave Lewis pictures of the smuggling, they would be able to say they had done what they could.

If they could do more, he intended to, though he couldn't imagine what more they could do aside from gathering photographic proof of what Sean Patricks was doing.

IN HUSHED TONES, AND through Facebook's messenger system after Edward was forced to return to his bedroom, Edward, Elizabeth, and Henri discussed what they were going to do. It wasn't an easy thing for them to figure out for there were many things to consider, not least of which was whether they should go against the punishment they had been given by Brenda and Lloyd and put themselves at risk for the third time in as many days.

Henri had no problem with the idea of them breaking their grounding. She was determined when it came to the matter of doing something to stop Sean Patricks and his gang of smugglers. The only question in her mind was how they were going to do it. Stop Patricks, that was. She didn't imagine that sneaking out was going to be all that difficult.

Edward leaned towards his cousin's way of thinking, though he didn't like the thought of disobeying Brenda and Lloyd, who had only punished them out of concern for their safety. He was in a similar position to Henri when it came to the question of how they could stop Sean Patricks. No matter how he wracked his brain, he couldn't think of a solution to that problem.

The obvious solution was to gather proof and take it to Constable Lewis, who would then be able to take appropriate steps. How they could gather proof without putting themselves at risk again, and without getting into more trouble, was a question he didn't have an answer to. Nor did he believe that gathering proof was going to be enough, given Constable Lewis' reluctance to believe them.

Elizabeth was by far the most conflicted. She wanted nothing more than to do the right thing, but she couldn't decide what the right thing was. As far as she could see, whatever they did, they would be doing something that was both right and wrong.

To stop Sean Patricks, or at least get proof against him, they would have to break the punishment Brenda and Lloyd had given them, but if they stuck to the punishment, they would be allowing Sean Patricks to get away with breaking the law.

26

"I'm sorry!" Elizabeth called out as she slammed the larder door and quickly propped a chair under the handle, effectively locking Brenda in.

She didn't like what she had done. She especially didn't like that she had been the one who had to do it, but there had been no choice. Since she was the one given the job of helping to prepare dinner, she had been elected to come up with a way of them getting out of there without Brenda stopping them, so they could do what they had, after much discussion, decided was the right thing.

"Let me out," Brenda shouted as she banged on the heavy door of the larder. "You let me out this instant, Elizabeth Bligh." Another bang shook the door. She was small, but decades of farming had given Brenda a wiry strength. "This is not how you treat people."

"I'm sorry," Elizabeth called through the door again before hurrying away. The longer she lingered there, the greater the temptation to release Brenda, which she knew would only get her into even more trouble than she already was.

"Come on," she shouted up to Edward and Henri, both of whom appeared at the top of the stairs quickly enough to make it clear they had been waiting just out of sight.

"What did you do with her?" Edward asked when he reached the bottom of the stairs. He could hear Brenda banging and shouting from the kitchen, but he didn't want to go down the passage to see what was going on.

"I shut her in the larder." The look of distress on Elizabeth's face made it plain how upset she was over what she had done.

Henri smiled reassuringly and patted Elizabeth on the arm. "It'll be alright. Lloyd'll be home in a bit, he'll let her out."

"We're going to be in so much trouble," Elizabeth moaned as she allowed her brother to lead her from the house. "I'm going to be in so much trouble."

Edward continued to guide Elizabeth out of the house and across the yard. "It had to be done," he said, liking the situation no more than his sister did. "We decided that. It'll all work out, so long as we're successful." The last was added almost in an undertone. They were going to be in trouble no matter what happened, he realised that, but if they were successful in getting the proof they were after they would at least be able to justify their actions.

Once they were out of the yard, the trio turned so they could head for the tunnel and the start of their descent towards the darkness of Sean Patricks' smuggling lair. They didn't know if James was ahead or behind them, or even if he had managed to get out of his house successfully, but they couldn't afford to simply wait around for him at the farm. Doing so would only lead to them being caught by Lloyd.

"YOU MANAGED TO GET away then," James said with a relieved smile when he joined the cousins at the tunnel, where they had been waiting for twenty minutes.

It had been easy for him to bravely declare that he was prepared to go alone to the caves to get the proof they had lost that morning while talking on Facebook. It was another thing altogether to actually do it, and he was glad his friends were there, though he hoped his decision to go wasn't going to end with one of them getting hurt, or all of them in too much trouble.

"How did you manage it?"

"Lizzie shut Brenda in the larder," Henri said, amused both by the look of surprise on James' face and the renewed look of distress on

Elizabeth's.

James looked at Elizabeth for several long moments before he found his voice. "You shut Brenda in the larder? How did she take that?"

"Not well," Elizabeth admitted unhappily. "She was yelling to be let out when we left. I'm going to be in so much trouble when we get back." She imagined all manner of horrific punishments being inflicted upon her once they returned to the farm, each worse than the one before it. She had never done anything like what she had done to Brenda before, she had never even considered such an act, and now she had she felt rotten. "I should never have agreed to get Brenda out of the way so we could leave."

"Stop worrying so much," Henri told her cousin. "You didn't hurt Brenda, you just shut her in a small room. She'll be fine. I'm sure Lloyd will be home soon and will let her out. Besides, it's not like it wasn't for a good cause. Speaking of which, we'd better get going if we're going to make it out before either the tide comes back in or night falls."

Without another word, Henri turned and slipped into the tunnel, so she could make her way through to the path on the other side of it. The path was in shadow as the sun headed for the Western horizon on the other side of the island, but it was still warm. Briefly, she considered taking off the denim jacket she was wearing but decided against doing so since her main reason for wearing it was as protection against injuring herself, not as a means of keeping warm.

She had already made it more than a dozen feet down the path, moving with as much haste as prudence allowed, when the others caught up to her.

Nothing was said as they all moved at the best pace they could manage on the uneven, downward slope. None of them wanted to take any longer about what they were doing than necessary.

They all realised that the more time they took, the greater the likelihood of the tide trapping them in the cave. If that happened, they would almost certainly be found by the smugglers when they conducted their illicit business.

The tide had not fully gone out when they reached the narrow beach at the foot of the path. It had receded enough for it to be relatively safe for them to keep going, however, even if it did result in them getting wet feet, for the second time that day.

As uncomfortable as wet socks and feet made them all, none of them said anything, let alone voiced any complaints. From the moment they began the descent they had, by unspoken agreement, kept all conversation to a minimum.

They were reasonably confident that Sean Patricks and his gang of smugglers would not be there yet, nonetheless, they didn't want to do anything that might draw attention to their presence in case they were wrong.

The knowledge of where they were going enabled them to move quicker than they had that morning, and it took them less than five minutes to reach the outer cave. Moments later, their footsteps guided by the beams from the torches they were, with the greatest reluctance, using to light their way, they left the pool behind to start along the tunnel that led into the cliff.

"I haven't seen any sign of my phone," Elizabeth said in a disappointed, and quiet, voice as they bypassed the first of the caves being used as storerooms. The others had told her she was almost certainly wasting her time, but she hadn't been able to resist scrutinising every inch of ground they passed over for some sign of her phone.

From the front of the group Edward, who had taken over the lead as soon as there was enough space for him to pass Henri, shushed his sister. Now that they were in the smugglers' den, it was even more important that they avoided making noises where they could.

They were creeping along, all but tiptoeing like burglars in a cartoon, yet they were still making too much noise for his liking.

He was sure that every faint scrape of a trainer on a loose stone could be heard at the other end of the tunnel, wherever that might be. He was equally sure that at any moment they were going to trigger an alarm, or Sean Patricks and his gang were going to jump out of the darkness to take them all prisoner.

Such was Edward's state of anxiety that he nearly went straight past the second cave, which seemed to be ten times farther away from the first cave than it had been that morning. If Henri hadn't been on his heels and paying attention, he would have missed it. As it was, he nearly jumped out of his skin when she put a hand on his shoulder to stop him.

It was almost a minute before the beating of his heart returned to a normal rate and he felt able to continue with what they were there to do.

"Here, you hold the torches," Edward told his sister, "while we take pictures."

Elizabeth took the torches and shone them around as instructed so she could provide enough light for the other three to take pictures and video of the cave's contents.

It had been Edward's suggestion that all three of them record what they found. He figured it was unlikely they would all lose their phones before they made it safely to Constable Lewis with their proof.

"What's up?" Edward asked of his sister when she surprised them by swinging the torches away from the boxes they were recording.

"Is that what I think it is?" Elizabeth asked in a frightened voice as she aimed the torches at the rear wall of the cave above their heads. The twin beams of light illuminated a device that had been fixed to the wall and aimed at the cave's entrance.

Edward found himself robbed of both movement and speech as he took in the small lens and even smaller red light, which indicated the device was in operation. It seemed like ages, though in reality, it was only a few seconds before he recovered. Movement returned before speech and he nodded in a dumbstruck manner.

"It's a camera," he said needlessly when he finally found his voice.
By then they had all realised what it was they were looking at. "We'd
better get out of here."

Elizabeth's thinking was ahead of her brother's and the words were
barely out of his mouth when she made for the entrance. She wasn't
running, only because there was neither the time nor space for her to
build up to a run, but she was moving quickly, too quickly to stop when
a light, brighter and more powerful than that from the torches she held,
blazed in her face.

She bounced off whoever was holding the light and would have
landed on her bum if Edward hadn't been behind her and able to catch
her.

"Leaving so soon, but you've only just got here."

The voice that came from behind the torchlight was low and
menacing and unrecognisable, though the teens guessed who it
belonged to — Sean Patricks. Since he was, as far as they knew, the
one in charge of the smugglers, it made sense that he would be the one
doing the talking.

Knowing who had most likely caught them did not make them feel
any better.

"Let's have some light in here," Patricks said over his shoulder. "We
want to see our guests properly, and I'm sure they'd like to be able to see
us."

Before the teens could wonder what Patricks meant, let alone what
he had in mind for them, a low rumbling sound started up. A few
seconds later, lights blazed on in the cave.

They were all dazzled by the sudden light, and by the time they
had recovered enough to see that the light was coming from a series of
high-powered lamps fitted flush into the ceiling, they had been herded
into the middle of the cave and surrounded.

They were outnumbered, six to four, but even if they hadn't been, they would have thought twice about trying to make a run for it. The men surrounding them were all at least four inches taller than Edward, which made them a head taller than Henri, who was the shortest of the teens, and much bulkier. Any one of them could have subdued two of the teens with ease, so trying to escape would almost certainly result in them being hurt.

"Well, that's better, isn't it," Patricks said in a voice that managed to be pleasant and friendly while at the same time containing an air of menace. "We can all see one another, rather than skulking around in the dark, hiding behind torches." He smiled at the teens, but without warmth.

"What are you going to do with us?" Edward asked, placing a restraining hand on Henri's arm, in case she was foolish enough to try something. He could feel the tenseness in her muscles, as though she was about to leap to the attack.

"Nothing, for now. It's too early in the day to do anything that might draw attention to us," Patricks said. "Well, when I say nothing, we will have to tie you all up. We have work to do before high tide, and I'd rather not have to waste men unnecessarily keeping an eye on you. You've already caused me enough problems for one day.

"I wanted to get things done out of the way this morning because I had plans for this afternoon. Thanks to your visit this morning, I had to cancel those plans and take risks I'm not happy about."

"How do you know we were here this morning?" Henri wanted to know. "That could have been anyone."

"Could have been, but wasn't," Patricks said. From his pocket, he took out an object that all four teens recognised after a brief period of bemused scrutiny as Elizabeth's phone. "When I investigated the racket you all made during your departure, I found this. Which is why there's now a camera in here, and I had my men come over early, to catch you when you came back, as I was sure you would."

"That phone could be anyone's," Elizabeth said.

"You know, you really are a terrible liar," Patricks told her. "It's locked, so I can't do anything with it, apart from this." He pressed the power button, which made the screen light up and reveal a picture of Elizabeth and Edward. "But that's enough to tell me the phone belongs to one of you. Which one doesn't really matter." To his men, he said, "Tie them up, tight, and take their phones, and anything that could be used as a weapon. I don't want them escaping or doing anything stupid. And when you're done with that, take them into the other cave out of the way."

None of the smugglers expected resistance from a bunch of teenagers, especially when two of them were girls, so they were relaxed as they moved forward to follow their orders. They were mistaken, as they soon discovered.

Elizabeth was scared out of her wits and made no effort to resist as she was grabbed, her hands pulled behind her back, and her wrists tied together with rope.

Edward remained quiescent as well. He wasn't as scared as his sister, though he was more scared than he could remember being, but he was worried that any resistance from him would result in the others being hurt. He didn't want to be responsible for that.

Neither Henri nor James felt the same way as Edward. They didn't know what Patricks had planned for them once he finished his business that night, but they weren't naïve enough to think that he was simply going to let them go.

Since they weren't inclined to wait to find out what was going to be done with them, let alone simply accept their fate, they both took action.

Henri attacked the first man to touch her, lashing out at him with all her fury. The man was surprised by the attack and before he could react, she raked her fingernails across his arm and cheek, drawing blood. She didn't settle for simply scratching him, she kicked and punched him as well.

Even when another of the smugglers grabbed her from behind, pinning her arms to her sides and lifting her off her feet, she didn't stop fighting. If anything, it made her kicks more effective since she could now reach higher with her feet.

One kick caught the smuggler in front of her on the side of the jaw, rocking his head to the side, though that hurt him less than it made him angry. Before she could kick out again, she was hit on the head. There was a sharp pain, and everything went black as she slumped in the arms of the man who held her.

While Henri's attack was thwarted quickly and easily, James' was more successful. He saw Sean Patricks turn away, clearly confident that his men could handle the teens, and took advantage of the opportunity.

Evading the thuggish smuggler who tried to grab him, he threw himself at Patricks. He grabbed Elizabeth's phone from Patricks', slipped away from the grasping hand that reached for him, and darted from the cave.

Instead of turning to his right, so he could head back the way he had come and escape, he turned to his left as he exited the cave.

By the time realised his mistake it was too late. He couldn't turn around and go back because Patricks was between him and the way to the cliff path, and he rated his chances of getting past the big man again at just about zero.

Instead of attempting the impossible, he kept going and hoped he would be able to find his way to Patricks' access into the tunnel. It was a risk since it was possible there were more members of the smuggling gang there, but a risk he had to take.

27

"Are you okay?" Edward asked of Henri when he saw she had woken. He was concerned about Elizabeth as well, but she hadn't been hit, while Henri had.

"I'll be fine," Henri said. With her hands tied behind her back, she couldn't check, but she suspected she was going to end up with a large lump where she had been hit. "Do you think James managed to get away?" He wasn't with them, so she assumed he must have, though she supposed he could have been caught and put somewhere else.

Edward didn't answer straight away, he was too busy straining to hear what was going on beyond their prison. He could hear nothing to suggest one way or another what had happened to James, though.

"Hopefully," he said finally. "I'm sure if they'd caught him, he'd have been put in here with us." He knew he was being optimistic, and the odds were against James, but just then optimism was all he had. "I'm sure he'll be back soon, with help."

"I hope he doesn't take too long," Henri said in a forced calm voice as she began struggling against the rope that bound her wrists together. It was tight and chafed at the skin, but she was determined to get free, even if it cost her to do so.

She wanted to believe that James would succeed in getting away and would soon return with help, but she thought it best not to simply sit back and wait for that to happen.

While Henri worked to free herself, Edward shifted his position. It was slow going, with his ankles as well as his wrists bound, but after several minutes, and what seemed like an enormous amount of effort, he managed to manoeuvre himself around until he was alongside his silent sister.

He couldn't hug Elizabeth, which was what he wanted to do, but he hoped that simply being next to her, shoulder to shoulder, would comfort her. She hadn't spoken a word since spotting the camera and he was concerned about her.

The three of them sat silently in the dim light which came from the one torch, resting on a box, they had been left as a courtesy by one of the smugglers.

For more than five minutes the only sounds to be heard were those made by Henri's attempts to get free. She had abandoned her efforts to pull her hands from the rope that secured her wrists, and her efforts to undo the knots, and was now trying to cut through her bonds by rubbing them against a rough protrusion she had found.

She hadn't made much progress, but she was unwilling to give up. If it took her all night to get free, she was prepared to work at it all night.

"We shouldn't have come."

Edward was startled by the sudden comment from Elizabeth. She had shown no sign of speaking before then, but he took it as a good sign, a sign that she was recovering from the fear and paralysis that had afflicted her since their capture.

"We shouldn't have come," Elizabeth repeated. "Now we won't even get back to the farm to be punished for shutting Brenda in the larder." Just then she would have welcomed being punished for that. Anything would be better than their current situation.

"I know," Edward said unhappily. "But it's going to be alright." He rested his head on his sister's shoulder, hoping to impart a little more reassurance to her. He could have done with some reassurance himself, but his sister needed it more.

28

James couldn't have said how long he had been running for before he collided with the wall of the tunnel; the darkness that surrounded him robbed him of all sense of time.

Since he couldn't see so much as a hand in front of his face, he had no idea if he had run into a dead-end, or if he had reached a point where the tunnel changed directly sharply.

From somewhere behind him he could hear the lumbering, echoing footsteps of the man chasing him. He didn't know how far away the man was, but the knowledge that the man was there somewhere was enough to keep his heart racing and make him desperately search the rock face in front of him with his hand.

He found an opening in the wall and spread his hands apart, searching for the other side of it and the top. He didn't want to move forward without first making sure it was an opening and not just a recess.

Once he was certain he wasn't going to walk straight into the wall again he set off up the new tunnel he had found.

His legs ached after nearly fifteen minutes of moving as quickly as he could, bumping along the tunnel as it twisted and turned. He had no idea how far he had come, or how much farther he had to go before he could escape the darkness that held him in its grasp. He didn't even know if he had gone the right way, or if he was going to find himself at a dead end.

Every time he thought about stopping, the faint glimmer of light from the torch carried by his pursuer pushed him on.

The light was too week to provide him with any guidance, but strong enough to remind him that danger was not far away, and it kept him going when all he wanted to do was stop and rest his aching muscles, even if only for a few moments.

The other thing that kept him going was the thought of his friends. They were in the hands of the smugglers and were relying on him to get help. He was the only hope they had.

Another — he didn't know how long — passed and then he stumbled as his legs finally gave out on him. Even then he didn't stop, as much as he wanted to. Since he couldn't get back to his feet he stayed on his hands and knees and crawled, knowing that it couldn't be long before he was caught now that his speed had slowed so drastically.

Things got worse for James when his knuckles banged against a rocky wall, drawing blood, which he licked away.

The wall he had hit was ahead of him, and he felt an upwelling of frustration as he searched it with his hands. Left and right and up and down he searched, scraping his hands constantly as he tried desperately to find a way past the obstacle that was blocking his escape.

A glance over his shoulder was enough to tell him that his pursuer was getting closer. He was still far enough back down the tunnel that James couldn't see past the light to make out even the outline of the man, but the distance to the light was less than it had been and that made him more desperate.

Ignoring the pain in his legs, he pushed himself to his feet so he could search higher, his hands going over every inch of the barrier that prevented his escape. He could find no sign of an opening, no matter how small, and he was on the verge of giving up in despair when he felt something move under his fingers.

He examined the area carefully, wishing he could see it, and discovered a small stone that could be pushed.

His imagination flared as the stone receded at his touch. Indiana Jones films and others of a similar nature, and the secret doors and passages that were always found, filled his thoughts, which expanded when he heard a click and felt the wall of the tunnel move under his hands. It was a door, of sorts.

As unbelievable as it seemed, someone, he assumed it was Solomon Kierney, had made a door to hide a part of the tunnel. He was sure it had been done because the hidden section led to the outside, and he felt a surge of relief as he found the edge of the door and pulled it open.

The moment he was through the gap, he took hold of the door's edge again and tugged at it. When he felt it move, he let go and left it to swing shut; he didn't fancy getting his fingers caught. Another injury was the last thing he needed.

He leant against the side of the hidden passage then to catch his breath. He didn't doubt that his pursuer was still getting closer, but he hoped Sean Patricks' accomplice would not look for him in there, assuming he would not have found the concealed door and would instead search elsewhere for him.

Hopeful he might be, but stupid he wasn't.

He allowed himself to rest for only a few moments before moving off again. This time, though, he took his phone from his pocket, so he could turn on the torch and illuminate his way, which he hadn't been willing to do before out of fear that the light would reveal his location.

The phone didn't provide him with as much light as a proper torch, but it did ensure that he wouldn't be bumping into any more walls and causing himself more harm.

He hadn't gone far when muffled curses told him his pursuer had reached the dead-end and was now trying to work out where he had gone.

29

When the rope securing her wrists parted, it did so with a suddenness that surprised Henri. She had been working the rope against the sharp rock she had found for an interminable period and had begun to give up hope of ever getting free.

She experienced a surge of relief, which was quickly pushed aside by a wave of pain as blood returned to her wrists and hands and she became aware of just how much she had hurt herself in getting free.

She rubbed herself vigorously to fully restore the circulation and then examined her injuries in the light from the torch. Several layers of skin had been rubbed away on either wrist, leaving her with bloody areas that stung, and she had bruised and scraped her knuckles and palms repeatedly.

The injuries were painful and annoying, though not as serious as she had first thought, so she put them from her mind and focused on freeing her ankles.

The knots were tough, but after a few minutes of work, during which she swore enough times that even her parents would have told her off, she managed to undo them.

She was still in a cave, with smugglers nearby, but she felt a lot better about her situation now that she could move around. She didn't allow herself to relax, however, there wasn't time for that.

Her movements awkward as the blood returned to her feet, she made her way to where Edward and Elizabeth sat, still shoulder to shoulder.

"I'll have you free in a moment," she said, moving around behind her cousins so she could begin working on the knots that bound Edward's wrists.

"Don't worry about us," Edward told her, even as he shifted about, trying to make it easier for Henri to free him. "We'll be fine. Get out of here, go and get help. We need you to get to the farm and call Constable Lewis in case James wasn't able to."

"I can't just leave you here," Henri protested."

"You have to. One of them could come in here at any moment. You should go now, while you can. We'll be alright."

A noise from somewhere outside the cave overcame Henri's reluctance to leave her cousins. She didn't want to go, but she realised Edward was right. They couldn't be sure James had got away safely, or that he was on his way back with help. They had to consider the possibility that he had been caught or injured while fleeing through the cliff.

It was better for her to go for help while she could than it was for her to stay and get caught trying to free Edward and Elizabeth.

A second noise, as unidentifiable as the first, had her on her feet and heading for the cave's entrance. She stopped for a moment to look back at her cousins and give them a reassuring smile, then she left, stepping into the darkness that filled the tunnel.

She was thankful that the route to the cave with the pool, and the outside world, was almost straight and she didn't have to take any side tunnels to get there. She didn't fancy trying to make her way through a maze in such darkness.

With one hand on the wall of the tunnel to keep her from stumbling into it and hurting herself, she moved as quickly as she felt it was safe to do. All the while, she worried she had been out of it for long enough that the tide had come in and would prevent her from escaping up the path to the top of the cliff.

If that proved to be the case, she wasn't sure what she would do. There had to be another way out of the tunnels, one that Sean Patricks used to get to his house, but since she didn't have a clue how to find that exit, and looking for it would require her to go back past Patricks and his gang, she hoped the tide was still out.

The moment she reached the pool and the cave it filled Henri saw that luck was not on her side. The tide was coming in. It had not yet come in enough to keep her from escaping, however, for which she was grateful.

She hurried along the narrow shelf that ran around the outside of the pool until she reached the entrance to the cave. She hesitated there for a moment and then plunged into the water, which reached halfway to her knees.

The water was cold and sent a shiver through her, but she ignored it and focused on placing her feet carefully to be sure she didn't slip on the stones beneath the water. The last thing she needed just then was a battle to avoid being drowned by the incoming tide.

Once out of the cave, Henri kept close to the cliff so she could use it to keep herself on her feet. It meant she got wetter than she would have liked as the incoming tide sprayed up from the cliff face to soak her from her hair on down, but she paid it no mind, except for when the water got in her eyes.

She was glad when she finally reached the path that ascended the face of the cliff for the tide was coming in quicker than she had thought.

By the time she got there the water had reached her knees, and she was becoming slower with every step.

With a sigh of relief, she finally got herself out of the water. She wanted to stop and rest for a moment but realised she couldn't afford to. Every second she delayed increased the chances of the sun dropping below the horizon before she could get to the top of the cliff.

If that happened, she was in real danger of missing her step and falling from the path, which was the last thing she wanted. As it was, she was so focused on watching where she was placing her feet, to be sure she didn't fall, that she didn't see the obstacle in front of her until she bumped into it.

She bounced off the obstacle and stumbled backwards. Her foot slipped out from under her, and she flailed her arms to try and regain her balance. She could feel herself starting to fall when something caught at the front of her t-shirt and hauled her upright.

It was several moments, during which her heart thudded loudly in her chest, before she realised the something that had grabbed her t-shirt was a hand. That realisation didn't reassure her. If anything, it made her heart beat more rapidly. She was certain she had been caught by either Sean Patricks or one of his smugglers.

She struggled violently against the hand that gripped her, despite the risk that she would fall if she did manage to get herself free, and only stopped when the owner of the hand spoke.

"Calm down, Henri. Henri, calm down, it's Lloyd." He let go of her only when he was sure she had stopped struggling and was no longer in danger of falling off the path to the surf below. "Where's Edward and Elizabeth?" he asked. "Are they alright? Did they manage to get away as well?"

"They're back there," Henri said, waving a hand vaguely over her shoulder without realising what it was Lloyd had said. "Patricks' got them tied up in a cave." Her heart continued to thud loudly in her chest. It slowed as her panic faded but didn't subside entirely, for she couldn't get over her concern for her cousins.

"Are they alright?" Lloyd asked again.

Henri shrugged. "They were alright when I left them, I suppose," she said. "We need to get help, Patricks' there with six of his smugglers, and they're waiting for more to turn up so they can shift some cargo. God knows what they'll do with Edward and Lizzie when they're done.

"Have you seen James?" she asked suddenly, as it occurred to her to wonder how Lloyd came to be there, though she realised almost immediately that it made sense for Lloyd to be there. It was obvious that the cave was where they would have gone after shutting Brenda in the pantry.

"Yes." Lloyd nodded. "He arrived at the farm a short while ago. It seems he found the secret tunnel under the ruins of Kierney's house. He told us what happened — we'll discuss what you all did later, now isn't the time — and convinced us to come with him to rescue you all."

"Where is he?" Henri looked past Lloyd for some sign of her friend but couldn't see him. "He isn't hurt, is he?"

"No, he's fine. He's leading Constable Lewis and the others through the tunnels from Kierney's house. I said I'd come this way and check it out." He gestured for Henri to turn around and head back the way she had come.

He would have preferred her to carry on up to the top of the cliff, where she would be safe, but given the narrowness of the path, there was no way for them to safely exchange places. If he was going to get to the bottom of the path, Henri would have to go first.

It wasn't until they moved off the steps and into the still-rising tide that Lloyd realised how deep the water was. It was above his knees, which meant it reached halfway up Henri's thighs.

"We'd better go back," he said, stopping the moment he saw how far up Henri's legs the water was. "It's too deep for us to go this way."

"We have to," Henri said, shivering as the water soaked into her muscles. "We have to rescue Edward and Lizzie."

Without waiting for Lloyd, she began slogging through the deepening water towards the cave she had escaped from just a short time before.

"You said others," Henri said when she had reached the safer ground of the shelf that ran around the interior of the cave and Lloyd had joined her. "Who's with James and Constable Lewis?"

"Father Jacobs, and some police officers he brought with him from the mainland."

Henri had expected to hear that it was some of the men from Blighton, not police officers from the mainland. "How come Father Jacobs brought police over?" she asked.

She remembered he had said he would help them with the smuggling situation if he could, but it seemed too coincidental for her to believe the police were on the island because of that.

"There isn't time to get into this now. If we're going to rescue Edward and Elizabeth before anything happens to them, we need to get moving." Lloyd was chilled by the water and keen to get moving before the cold seeped into his muscles and rendered him useless, not that he thought he stood much chance against Sean Patricks and his gang of smugglers anyway, not on his own.

30

"How much further is it?" Constable Lewis puffed the question as he hurried along the tunnel, the light from the torch in his hand focused on James, who was leading the group.

The echoing footsteps of Father Jacobs and the five policemen he had brought with him from Handley, who were hard on his heels, almost drowned his words and he had to repeat them to be sure James had heard him.

"I'm not sure," James called back over his shoulder without slowing. "Can't be far to the main passage now, though." He saw no reason to keep his voice down to avoid alerting the smugglers to their approach, the group behind him were making enough noise to alert someone hard of hearing.

When the first cry of alarm came, James realised that the distance from the storage cave to where he had run into the wall was shorter than he had thought.

Fortunately, and he was glad it was the case, the passage from the ruins of Kierney's house, where he had found himself after finally climbing out of the confines of the cliff what seemed like an eternity ago, held no turns, deviations, or secondary tunnels branching off into the darkness. If there had been, he wasn't sure he would have known which direction to take, and he suspected he would have got them all lost long before they found Edward, Elizabeth, and Henri.

EDWARD AND ELIZABETH huddled closer together as they tried to interpret the noises that reached them. The way the noises echoed back and forth through the tunnel outside the cave made it impossible for them to be sure of what was going on, but they both concluded that either James or Henri had managed to escape and had returned with help.

When a figure appeared in the entrance to the cave, Edward's first and hopeful thought was that it was one of the rescuers, come to set them free. As the figure moved further into the cave, and the light from the torch illuminated their face, he saw that it was not a rescuer, it was Sean Patricks.

The anger visible on Patricks' face made Edward go cold with fear. His fear grew when he saw the knife in Patricks' hand, and if it hadn't been for his determination to stay strong for his sister, it might have overwhelmed him.

"Stay away from us," Edward said as forcefully as he could when Patricks approached the spot where he and Elizabeth were tied up.

"Shut up." Patricks struck Edward a backhanded blow that knocked him over and left him struggling to get back up. "You kids have cost me, badly. I picked this place because the local copper was too stupid and lazy to cause me any problems. Why did you brats have to get involved? Now I've got to relocate. You should have kept your noses out of things that don't concern you," he snarled as he bent to slip the blade of his knife under the rope securing Elizabeth's ankles. With one quick slice, he freed her legs and then yanked her to her feet. "I just wish I had the time to deal with you as you deserve."

"Let her go," Edward called after Patricks while he continued his efforts to right himself.

He was ignored and could only watch in despair as his sister was led away, to he knew not what fate. Desperately, he fought against his bonds, but all he accomplished was the removal of another layer of skin, which left him bleeding more than he had been already.

Elizabeth was too scared to do anything more than make a series of unintelligible sounds that were a mix of fear and pain as she was dragged from the cave. Even if she hadn't been paralysed by thoughts of what was going to happen to her, she would have been hard-pressed to put up any resistance with her hands bound behind her back.

CHAOS. THAT WAS THE only word to describe what was happening in the caves and tunnels.

The police and the smugglers were evenly matched. The police had batons and were trained in their use, but the tight quarters, lack of decent lighting, and equal numbers negated most of the advantage the batons might have otherwise provided.

The result was chaos as the police strove to subdue the smugglers and put them in handcuffs, and the smugglers fought to get away, using whatever they could lay their hands on as weapons.

While the police and the smugglers fought, James ducked and dodged his way through the bigger bodies and went looking for his friends. He was determined to rescue them, having got them into the situation with his talk of smugglers and smuggling, and his desire to prove he wasn't lying.

He could think of only two places where Edward, Elizabeth, and Henri might be, assuming nothing serious had been done with them — the two storage caves.

The first cave was empty; of his friends at least. It was still full of boxes, some of which had been partly unpacked. Since he could see that his friends weren't there from the entrance, he didn't waste time entering the cave. Instead, he made for the second cave, where he was sure he would find them.

He was still a distance from the cave when he encountered Elizabeth. She was being forced along the passage by Sean Patricks, who held her tight by the arm as he pushed her ahead of him.

Patricks stopped at the sight of James, who was little more than a silhouette in the dim light from the distant and dancing torches.

"Out of my way, boy," he snarled menacingly.

James stopped. He couldn't see clearly what Patricks was holding to Elizabeth's throat, but he didn't need to. He could guess what it was, and that was enough to make him hold back. He had no desire to do anything that would cause Patricks to hurt Elizabeth, especially when there were others with him better suited to deal with the situation.

"Hey!"

The sudden shout from behind him made Patricks turn sharply towards the new threat. As he did the blade of the knife left Elizabeth's throat and his grip on her arm loosened.

Elizabeth remained too shocked by everything that had happened to take advantage of the situation. She stood there, scared, and immobile, even though one quick move might have freed her.

Fortunately, James wasn't paralysed by panic. The moment he saw the flash of light off metal as the knife blade left his friend's throat, he leapt forward. He had no weapon, something that didn't occur to him until he was already in motion, but by then it was too late for him to worry about the lack.

He reached for Patricks' right hand, the one in which the knife was held, and fixed onto it, using his weight, which was barely enough for the job, to lever the weapon further away from Elizabeth.

He continued to hang on grimly, using all his strength, even after Patricks released Elizabeth. He had attacked simply to get Elizabeth free, but he realised that if he let go of Patricks, he would almost certainly find himself in more danger than he was just then. He didn't fancy that, so he clung on, fighting to keep the smuggler from freeing up the knife that had already come dangerously close to his skin a few times.

He didn't know whose call had provided the distraction that had enabled him to attack, the echoing effect of the tunnel had rendered the voice difficult to recognise, but he suspected it was Lloyd. He couldn't imagine who else could have approached from that end of the tunnel.

Whoever it was, and he hoped it was Lloyd, James prayed that they would come to his rescue, and soon. He didn't know how much longer he could keep Patricks from freeing his hand and gaining full use of the knife he held.

HENRI IGNORED LLOYD'S warning to slow down and continued to move quickly along the tunnel towards the cave where she had left Edward and Elizabeth.

Soon enough she reached the cave and darted inside, heedless of the possibility that there might now be someone in there, guarding her cousins.

Fortunately, her haste was not punished, but she still stopped abruptly when she saw that things were not as she had left them. Edward was still there and still bound, but he was alone. Of Elizabeth, there was no sign.

"Where's Lizzie?" Henri asked as she hurried over to Edward and dropped down beside him so she could begin working on the knots that kept him bound.

"He took her. Patricks," Edward said. "I don't know where. It was only a minute or so ago. He came in, so angry, and took her with him. It was just after we heard all the noise. What's going on? You haven't been gone long enough to get help." His words came out in a rush as his thoughts danced between relief at seeing his cousin and concern for his sister, whom he was sure was in more danger than any of them had ever imagined.

"James got away. He found Kierney's secret entrance, he escaped that way and got help," Henri said as she struggled to untie Edward. "I bumped into Lloyd as I was going up the cliff path." As she said that

Lloyd entered the cave, puffing a bit from the effort of trying to keep with her.

The relief Edward had felt at the return of Henri was nothing to what he felt when he saw Lloyd. He was still concerned for Elizabeth, but he couldn't help feeling his heart leap joyously at the sight of an adult, and friendly, face.

"Edward, you okay? Where's your sister?" Lloyd asked.

Without breaking step, he reached into his pocket for the knife he carried. He sank slowly and awkwardly to his knees when he reached Edward and opened the blade so he could slice away the rope that Henri had failed to undo.

With Lloyd now there to free Edward, who was recounting what had happened to Elizabeth, Henri left the cave to go in search of her cousin. It wasn't that she didn't trust Constable Lewis or the officers Father Jacobs had brought over from Handley to rescue Elizabeth, she just didn't feel right staying in the cave with Edward, when he was now safe, while Elizabeth was in danger.

Since she and Lloyd hadn't encountered Patricks and Elizabeth as they made their way up the tunnel, she concluded they must have gone the other way. Fortunately, the tunnel didn't deviate, so she didn't have to worry about missing them by taking a wrong turning, she just had to move quickly to catch them up.

The tunnel was dimly lit, almost dark, and she kept a hand on the wall beside her as she moved hurriedly through it in pursuit of her cousin.

She hoped Elizabeth and her captor were not far ahead, but she had no way of knowing since there was too much noise echoing through the tunnel for her to make out anything that might have told her how close she was to her quarry.

It turned out she wasn't far behind them. Either that or she was moving much quicker than they were. She wasn't sure which it was, but she caught up to them sooner than she expected to. She might even have walked into them if she hadn't heard the snarling voice.

"Out of my way, boy."

Henri couldn't see past Patricks. Even if there had been more light, she wasn't sure she would have been able to, but she didn't need to. She could guess who Patricks was speaking to, James, she couldn't imagine who else he would be calling 'boy'.

"Hey," she called out to distract Patricks. Even to herself, her voice sounded wrong, louder and less feminine than usual, as the echoing effect of the tunnel distorted it. She was sure that was helpful, though, since Patricks was more likely to be distracted by a man's voice than by a girl's.

What followed was unclear. She saw the outline of Patricks turn towards her and then he stumbled and a figure, she assumed it was Elizabeth, fell at his feet.

It took her a moment to realise that Patricks hadn't stumbled, he had been attacked by James. It was brave of him to attack Patricks, Henri thought, but also foolhardy. Almost immediately, however, she realised that had she been in his position, she would have done the same thing to rescue Elizabeth.

She wanted to go to her cousin and make sure she was alright. She couldn't, though, because to get to Elizabeth, she would have to get past Patricks, and he was taking up most of the space in the tunnel as he fought with James.

Her next thought was to help James. She was sure it was just as foolhardy for her to attack Patricks as it had been for James to do so, but she had the advantage of doing so from behind. With luck, they would be able to keep the smuggler there until the police could arrive without getting hurt too badly.

She launched herself onto Patricks' back and flung her arms around his neck. She hadn't intended to choke him, she hadn't thought of anything beyond jumping onto his back, but that was what she ended up doing. Her arms tightened instinctively to keep her from falling off,

with the result that she squeezed his throat and caused him to struggle
for air.

She hung on for dear life as Patricks attempted to free himself so he
could breathe again.

When he threw himself back into the wall of the tunnel, squashing
her between him and it, she gasped in pain. She was determined not to
let go, however, not even when he repeated the move and she banged
her head hard on the wall, causing her to see stars.

Over Patricks' shoulder, Henri could see James clinging to his arm
the way she was clinging to his neck and back. She also saw an
occasional glint as the distant light from farther up the tunnel reflected
off something in Patricks' hand.

She fervently hoped that neither Elizabeth nor James had been
hurt with the knife and that she wouldn't be hurt with it either.

How long she and James struggled with Patricks for, she had no
idea, though she suspected it wasn't as long as it felt. All she knew for
certain was that it was a relief when Lloyd appeared to help them.

31

The kitchen of the Bligh farm was full to overcrowding.

Lloyd, Edward, James, and Henri, who had changed out of her soaking wet clothes and into her pyjamas and a thick and fluffy dressing gown, were seated around the table. The rest of the space was taken up by Father Jacobs, Constable Lewis and the Inspector who had led the police officers from Handley, who were escorting Sean Patricks and his smugglers to jail, while Brenda bustled about, providing everyone with hot drinks and homemade biscuits.

Despite the number of people in the room, conversation was almost non-existent.

Every one of them, even the inspector, who didn't know her, were waiting to hear about Elizabeth.

Only Constable Lewis, who tried repeatedly to justify his lack of either belief or action regarding the smugglers, spoke, and even he fell silent when it became clear that no one was interested in what he had to say.

It was almost twenty minutes before Doctor Preston came downstairs and entered the kitchen, where he found himself the focus of eight pairs of eyes.

If he found it disconcerting to be the centre of such attention, he showed no sign of it. He accepted the mug Brenda handed to him — she had run out of cups and saucers — took a sip of tea, and only then did he speak.

"She'll be fine," he told the room. "She's suffering from shock, which is no surprise given what she has apparently been through this evening, and the chances are she'll have some problems over the next few days. Nightmares, panic attacks, anxiety, cold shivers even when it's warm, loss of appetite, no energy, that kind of thing. It should pass, though.

"If the problems persist, it might be necessary for her to see a psychologist or someone, but I don't think it will come to that. For now, I've given her a sedative. She should sleep till morning. If she acts unexpectedly when she wakes up, or you're worried about anything, call me. Other than that, just give her whatever space or support she needs.

"As for Henrietta, you'll need to keep an eye on her, she shows no sign of the shock her cousin is suffering, but the shock may be delayed in her case. Other than being stiff for the next few days, needing the dressings on her hands and wrists checked regularly, and possibly waking up with a headache, she should be okay.

It was an indication of how much Henri hurt from being thrown into the tunnel wall while riding Sean Patricks' back that she did not object to the use of her full name.

Doctor Preston finished his tea and then left. He was curious to know what had been happening on the island, beyond the sparse details he had been given, especially since it involved officers from Handley. It was clear, though, that having dealt with both Elizabeth and Henri Bligh, who had needed her head checked, and whose back, hands, and wrists had needed treating, he had no more reason to be there.

He consoled himself with the thought that Constable Lewis' involvement in whatever was going on guaranteed that the story, albeit a distorted version of it, would soon be on its way around Blighton.

"I'm going to go and sit with Elizabeth for a while, make sure she's alright," Brenda said after seeing the doctor out, and leaving the others in the kitchen, she made her way upstairs.

The anger she had felt at being shut in the larder was gone, it had vanished the moment she heard that Elizabeth, Edward, and Henri had been caught by the smugglers, to be replaced by concern. That concern had increased when she saw the state the teens were in following their ordeal.

It was Henri who finally broke the silence. "So, who's going to tell us what happened?" she asked, looking around the kitchen. When nobody volunteered an answer, she turned to James. "Lloyd said you found the entrance to the tunnel under Kierney's house."

"Yeah." James nodded. "I went the wrong way when I escaped the cave, and after running into a wall," he reached a hand up to his face, which Brenda had treated while Doctor Preston was dealing with Henri and Elizabeth, "I found a secret door. The tunnel on the other side of it ended at a shaft with a ladder that led upwards. It came out through the bottom of the fireplace in the ruins of Kierney's house.

"I came straight here once I was out and found Constable Lewis already here. I was trying to convince him that you guys really had been grabbed by Patricks' smugglers, he didn't want to believe me even when I showed him the pictures of the boxes, when Father J turned up with the inspector and a bunch of officers from Handley. You didn't tell me where they came from, or how they came to be here," he said to the priest.

"I guess that's my cue to tell my part in tonight's little drama," Father Jacobs said with a smile, as if he had been waiting for just such an opportunity. "I said I'd help you guys if I could, and I have. I've spent some time over the past couple of days trying to find out what I could about Sean Patricks. I wasn't able to find out much, though, other than that he owns several bars and nightclubs with his brother.

"Fortunately, luck was on my side. The bishop asked to see me today, so I took the opportunity to see my nephew, Inspector Deakins, who works in Handley." He gestured unnecessarily to the inspector, whom Constable Lewis kept glancing at uneasily. "He agreed to find out what he could while I had my meeting with the bishop. When I returned, he told me that customs have been investigating Patricks on suspicion of smuggling and tax evasion.

"I was all set to come back and tell you guys that the situation was being handled, and there was no need for you to put yourselves at risk. Unfortunately, I didn't get a chance." He was unhappy that the teens had taken the risk they had and put themselves in danger, but relieved that things had not gone worse for them, though he realised that that was mostly down to luck. "It was only by chance that I rang home to check for messages and heard the one that James left me, telling me what had happened this morning, and what you were all planning for this evening."

Edward and Henri both turned to look at James. He hadn't told them he had left a message for Father Jacobs. He shrugged as if to say that the message had slipped his mind.

"The moment I heard it I called Paul and told him what was happening. It's just as well he's an inspector and able to make things happen. He made a few calls to arrange things and then brought me over with the officers he was able to get." The tea in the cup he was holding had been forgotten as he related the day's events and was now cold, as he discovered when he paused to take a sip. He grimaced and set the cup aside. "We went straight to James' when we reached the island and learned that he had already gone. Your father wasn't home, James, but your aunt was there, and she was in a panic. I think you should call and let her know that you're safe before she decides you're dead or something."

James looked abashed at the thought of the distress he had caused his aunt. "I'll do that now." He got up, so he could make his way out of the kitchen.

He didn't like to think about how much trouble he was going to be in when his dad found out what he had been up to. He had proved that he was neither a liar nor playing a prank on Constable Lewis, and he had been involved in the capture of a gang of smugglers, but he doubted his father would consider any of that as mitigation.

He took some consolation from the thought that though his father was unlikely to be impressed by what he had done, his friends would be. He looked forward to going back to school after the holidays so he could tell them all about him helping to catch smugglers. He smiled briefly at the thought of his friends' reactions.

The smile was wiped away the moment his aunt answered his call.

Father Jacobs took up his story again once James had left the kitchen. "After we discovered James was gone, we hurried out here, hoping to catch you all before you left to go to the cave. We were farther behind you than I thought, for you were already in the hands of the smugglers, and James had escaped and made it back here.

"Paul immediately took charge and James took us to the ruins of Kierney's house, where he showed us the hidden entrance to the tunnels and guided us through them to where you were. Thank goodness we were in time." He didn't like to think about what might have happened to the teens if they hadn't got there when they did.

Inspector Deakins stepped forward so he could speak then. "I'm sure you realise by now," he said, addressing Edward and Henri, "that you took an enormous, and very foolish, risk, both this morning and this evening. Especially this evening, when you knew the caves you discovered were being used by a gang of smugglers. You have all been extremely lucky. A few relatively minor injuries, a bit of a chill, and some shock. You could have ended up with worse, a lot worse."

Edward couldn't help thinking about what else might have happened to them and was extremely glad they had been so fortunate. At the same time, he chastised himself for the risks they had taken. He was the eldest of them and should have had enough sense not to put them in such danger.

Henri wasn't thinking about the danger they had been in or the injuries they had received. The danger was in the past, and the injuries would heal. She was thinking about the excitement of it all and, like James, was looking forward to going back to school, so she could tell her friends about helping to catch a gang of smugglers.

"That being said," Deakins continued, "I have to express my thanks for your willingness to get involved. Many people, even adults, would have chosen not to get involved, especially after being ignored by the local police, either out of fear or out of a desire not to put themselves out and cause themselves problems."

Constable Lewis looked distinctly uncomfortable at that and seemed to shrink back into the corner where he was standing, as if trying not to draw attention to himself.

"According to Customs and Excise, they didn't even suspect that Sean Patricks was using this island for his smuggling operation, they thought the operation was based on the mainland, so without your help, it might have been some time before he was caught."

"Does that mean we get a reward?" Henri asked eagerly. She didn't want money, though she was sure James would be glad of a financial reward, just something to acknowledge what they had done.

Deakins smiled. "I wouldn't want to encourage you to do anything like this again, but a reward of some kind might be appropriate. That will be for someone more senior than me to decide, though."

32

A huge grin on her face, Henri took the newspaper from Brenda and rushed upstairs. She burst into the bedroom and flung herself onto the bed, where Elizabeth remained after a poor night's sleep as a result of nightmares, stemming from the previous evening's ordeal.

"Look, we're heroes," she said excitedly, holding up the paper so Elizabeth could see the headline and the pictures, taken from their social media accounts.

CURIOUS COUSINS CATCH SUSPECTED SMUGGLERS

A trio of cousins, and their friend, are all to receive awards for bravery from the police in Handley after uncovering a smuggling ring on the tiny island of Bligh, where they were spending the holidays with family.

After hearing stories of the island's past, which included smuggling in the 1800s, the teens went exploring and discovered that modern-day smugglers were using the island's cave system.

When the local police on the island refused to believe them, the cousins and their friend set out to get proof and yesterday evening, in a terrifying ordeal, the teens came face to face with the smugglers and were captured, though one of them, James Allen, managed to escape and get help.

Full story on page 4

Henri read the story to Elizabeth, and then to Edward when he entered the bedroom.

She was so excited by the thought of getting an award from the police that she couldn't sit still. Getting up from the bed she paced around the room.

She had thought that spending the summer on Bligh Island with relatives she didn't know was going to be boring. So far it had proved to be anything but. She was glad of that, even if Edward and Elizabeth, especially Elizabeth, did look as though they would have preferred the anticipated boredom.

The rest of the holidays were bound to be a let-down after how they had started, but she hoped there would be some more excitement, though perhaps not as much danger.

THE END.

Don't miss out!

Visit the website below and you can sign up to receive emails whenever Alex R Carver publishes a new book. There's no charge and no obligation.

https://books2read.com/r/B-A-BNVD-TPJJB

BOOKS 2 READ

Connecting independent readers to independent writers.

Also by Alex R Carver

Cas Dragunov
An Unwanted Inheritance

Inspector Stone Mysteries
Where There's a Will
An Eye For An Eye
A Perfect Pose
Into The Fire
A Stone's Throw

The Curious Cousins
The Curious Cousins and the Smugglers of Bligh Island

The Oakhurst Murders
Written In Blood
Poetic Justice

Standalone
Exposed
Inspector Stone Mysteries Volume 1 (Books 1-3)
The Oakhurst Murders Duology

Watch for more at https://alexrcarver.wordpress.com/.

About the Author

After working in the clerical, warehouse and retail industries over the years, without gaining much satisfaction, Alex quit to follow his dream and become a full-time writer. Where There's A Will is the first book in the Inspector Stone Mysteries series, with more books in the series to come, as well as titles in other genres in the pipeline. His dream is to one day earn enough to travel, with a return to Egypt to visit the parts he missed before, and Macchu Picchu, top of his wishlist of destinations. When not writing, he is either playing a game or being distracted by Molly the Yorkie, who is greedy for both attention and whatever food is to be found.

You can find out more about Alex R Carver at the following links
https://twitter.com/arcarver87
https://alexrcarver.wordpress.com/
https://medium.com/@arcarver87
https://www.facebook.com/Alex-R-Carver-1794038897591918/
Read more at https://alexrcarver.wordpress.com/.